Life in an ever-shrinking box

Alisa Popova

Book design by Alisa Popova

Cover design courtesy of Alisa Popova, with assistance from Freja Salka Christine Werner and Dhairya Sanghavi

Publisher: BoD · Books on Demand, Strandvejen 100, 2900 Hellerup, bod@bod.dk
Print: Libri Plureos GmbH, Friedensallee 273, 22763 Hamborg, Tyskland
ISBN: 978-87-4305-934-9

Dedicated to Dhairya.

For supporting this book, and all my dreams.

Table of Contents

Just a bowl of rice

On hot, Thai island nights, when the sunset sprinkles mosquitoes through the pink clouds like pieces of confetti, the sounds of people are inescapable. Regardless of how far away they are, voices will linger in the heat and tempt you outside, even though it means falling mercy to the endless lines of bugs. When you lean into their call, hiking amidst the scratching weeds, your footsteps are not thunderous or monumental. They do not shake the soil or reverberate through the jungle. Instead, you hear the reactions of nature. The bending leaves and snapping sticks, making space for the feet of another human, guiding the human to more of their own.

Past the fields on the gravel road, rocks clatter against the metal of your bike and its wheels thrust against the paving. The continuous spinning of the wheel blends into that of a hundred others. Your ear catches the wheels of trucks, bikes and mopeds vibrating in unison, speeding and slowing with the flowing waves of traffic which direct you to your destination, as they do for many others. As the sun finally disappears, a thousand other lights flicker on, as if to say *the world is asleep, but we are not,* people shine their own little suns on each other.

When the market is near, the scent of noodles grows thick and grainy, the sound of them slurping and shaking sloppily, wet lumps squeaking against bowls and chopsticks. Spices seep into every pore. What good are thoughts here, when there is a ceaseless flow of new sensation calling to you? Your own mind is irrelevant here. Let it rest under the flashing street-food stalls. Let it feel gentle gusts break up hot sheets of humid air, wind painting your skin with peace. What good are thoughts when a bowl of rice is placed in your hands, vegetables sparkling like colourful gemstones, flavourful steam traversing the sky?

Breathe in, unable to distinguish each ingredient from the dish as a whole. There is no wheat, no vegetable, but rather a noodle and broth, elevated from what they once were. You are beyond the sum of your parts. Let the dish be an amalgamation of experiences, techniques and talents, passed down for generations and heavy with expectations. Let yourself be nothing more than a bowl of rice served at a noisy Thai market under the stars. Breathe. Enjoy.

Siren

Part I - The Future

Cuckoo.

A cuckoo's song gets carried by the wind, tying heart-shaped knots around rows of silver birch trees. Each tree stands perfectly straight, firm soldiers plucked up by invisible strings from the sky. The white birch is spotted like an army under a rain of blood and tears, commanded to hold a losing position. Beside lies a mossy brook, the flow of its river trapped in the past. It has snowed for many years, water unable to resist the ceaseless, violent freeze. Beneath its surface is a false sense of calm in the stillness of ice, so convincingly silent that the war around becomes easy to forget. All is covered in eternal frost, which has eroded the rocks into smooth, conforming stones of equal height and width. It burned away the grass' roots, so that the ground is a dotted mixture of black dirt and snow, patched like the hips of a cow. That is one of few semblances of life that still exist here, beside the trees, bare year-round. The ice does not allow for change, trapping the valley in the past eternally. The moss, the trees, they are long dead, but the freeze pretends that all is well, smoothing any cracks in its mirage with a white layer.

Today is a new day. Time is able to step forward for a forbidden moment. The song of the cuckoo has changed something, bringing light to the valley. The sun's breath caresses the glazed water, and the curved top of a human head protrudes from the river, followed immediately by teeth. The figure is a woman, head covered in tangled hair and face red from the rushing blood after an eternity embedded in ice. The woman bites and chews her way through the surface, tearing at it like wild meat. She is sharp, forged of steel and immune to pain from enduring the battering of centuries of waves. Before, in a past where life was a goal and not a given, she would have felt the pain. She is different now, forced to become strong and immovable.

While stuck below, she had been in a trance. Between sleep and waking, she endured nightmares of the apocalypse on repeat. The cuckoo's song broke through her jammed mind, shaking her out of the coma and imbuing a desire to be alive again. The weary spirit was summoned through hope of life's new beginning, that the valley may be revived and begin to grow into the beauty it once had.

Using her hands to rip through glaciated plates, she pulls her heavy body from the water. It is not easy, even for the sturdy woman. Her legs haven't fulfilled their purpose in a long time. They don't remember how. So she swivels her hips and stomach, using her arms to throw herself from the water in a protest of life, that she has not yet been destroyed. She looks around, how many years have passed since the trees have sung? How long must she still wait before her tongue is strong enough to pronounce home again, before her ears learn to decode the tune of fellow humans?

Now she sits where the brook and the dirt meet, her numb hips scratched by dried-up flower stems. Everything is preserved as it was before, she realises. The mountains are here, the river and the valley. All, seldom for the moving wilderness and its sounds. The crickets don't chirp, they lie instead, numb in the dirt. Unable to decay and return to the Earth or awaken and sing again. Everything is hard and spiked now. Where flowerbeds lay and trees blossomed, instead twigs poke out like knives dug into the land and sky. They, too, have been made violent by the cold.

Deep in a dormant core whispers a lingering hope that she may stand on the warm surface again, feeling her bruises blister in a joy of pain, that she would cry, and another person could cry with her. The trees would shake at each powerful movement as the woman, an animal once more, would climb the thick branches with her aching arms. Soreness as the body's message that it yet lives, this would suffice. All she wants is to feel something, even if it is unhappiness. She does not dare ask for laughter or joy as she has long forgotten it, forgotten how to be warmed by happiness. Instead, she waits for a feeling compatible with the frost, the cold environment. The absence of feeling has diluted her, numbness has chewed at her lungs, and she longs to sense a breathless rush again. So, she asks for hope from the wild, begs for a leaf to fall in the silent forest, that her numbness may cease and that she could learn to be free again.

Cuckoo.

The sound is heard once more. Her heart rushes to pump blood and adrenaline to each organ, understanding that the dream of life returning to her valley is real. She pushes herself through the dirt, legs limping behind her, breasts digging holes in the dirt as she propels the body forward, using the surge of strength that hope gifted her. Her torso bleeds from the tearing sticks, blood brown and dry as it struggles to flow. Her head darts around, scanning the trees and their dead branches for the silver-breasted cuckoo with its yellow beak. Faster, harder, she pushes herself forward, further now, through the aching pain which wakes the body. She remembers the familiar paths of the valley like outlines of her own veins, ready to uncover all the spaces where a bird might nest. Continuing forward, her body is alive and awake, and she smiles as her knees twitch and shake in glee. Electricity pulses through her, feet jerking and toes wiggling, suddenly imbuing her with enough force to push her entire body up. The woman gallops like a wild animal in the valley, generating wind flow from her rushing limbs and letting it catch onto her dark hair.

Cuckoo.

The sound is heard again while the woman uses her nails to scratch ice from the bark of a birch tree, trying to revive it so that it could enjoy the valley's returning life with her. As the sound reverberates, she remembers her goal and sets off running in its direction

Cuckoo.

At the base of a mountain lies a slim entrance to a cave. The noise beckons her inside carefully.

Cuckoo.

The cave is dim and murky, wet mud squelching under her heavy feet. She listens for the fluttering of a cuckoo's wings but receives only the song's echo. Why would the cuckoo be here, in the darkness? Why does it not seek light, or to meet the valley and remind it of beautiful life?

Cuckoo.

Silence. Then, a thump is heard. The woman lays in the cave's dirt, her body paralyzed. Her legs no longer work. Now, neither do her arms or head. She cannot remove herself from the cave, nor turn her neck away from the cuckoo. The only thing she can do is close her eyes.

A shriek is heard, the throat raw and frozen. It has not been used for a lifetime, and in this lifetime it will hear no response. It is now the woman's own gasps and sobs that echo through the forest. The trees are still and watchful in the distance, curiously detached from the morbid scene. She has discovered the lie now, too late to avoid bleeding false hope, red blood gushing for a resistant minute before solidifying into ice. She no longer burned hot, unable to resist the freeze. She'd let her guard down, a human moment after years of resilience. The frost finally managed to reach her heart.

The cuckoo's corpse is preserved by the frost, illuminated by a gentle ray of sun which had crawled into the cave. The body lacks the ugly appearance of old death, its eyes closed in acceptance as if it too, had predicted the coming apocalypse. Its song was a simple echo of the past, a trick of a foreign wind. It lies often, lacking regret, stealing memories and twisting songs of life into meaningless echoes. The woman is alone again in the valley. The barren trees do not shed a leaf in mourning for her. They simply have none left.

How long does it take for a dream to truly die?

Surely longer than the time it takes to bury one in the depths of the mind, and even that repression can stretch across lifetimes. It must be somewhere before the haunting thought of an alternate life draws its shadow over every moment. Before a person stands outside, staring at a horizon that has lost its colour, after realising it's too late, but before fully processing the weight. Long after certain announcements of *I can do this,* longer still after the doubt of whether they ever could. It's difficult to speak in absolutes when the illusion of something ahead still lingers, and perhaps that's why they don't notice that hope passed on until reaching out for a hand and finally seeing that it fled in their youth.

When everything changes, it doesn't always happen quickly, nor dramatically. Sometimes the hurt isn't a hot, lightning rage that zaps the body. Instead, it could be a constant drizzle, seeping through a leaky roof until an eventual realisation that the house hasn't been dry or warm in years. Sometimes, it's sitting in a quiet kitchen with a racing heartbeat, knowing that the plains and hills outside aren't trembling in fear. It's the understanding that the valley will forget you and learn to care for another, erasing a previously known and loved face from the history books, stories of people fading away.

If she knew her destiny, she might continue to lay by the hills, soaking in the comforting unknown for one, last, peaceful moment.

Now the woman is awake, truly. She never exited the water, never broke through the ice. Her hands were only powerful in her dreams. The only movement made now was the opening of mouth to scream, and her eyes to see the arctic water fill her mouth. Lungs cooled by the ice, she lets her dreams go, remembering a poem she'd read as a child.

> *An actor said his lines*
> *But the camera wasn't rolling.*
> *The phone ceaselessly rings*
> *Faded memories of a voice calling.*
> *Tree stump stands strong*
> *Never able to regrow.*
> *Will you remember my world,*
> *When it gets covered in snow?*
> *Ash of bullets and bombs*
> *Particles in the air*
> *Infinite expressions of love,*
> *Hidden,*
> *No longer there.*
> *I believe in yesterday.*
> *I want to cherish its views.*
> *But my grief is perpetual*
> *As I don't yet know what else*
> *I will lose.*

Part II - The Past

Someone calls my name, a calm, sweet melody undisturbed by the windless atmosphere. The reverberation of a familiar tongue, human buzzing my direction to reveal a word I hadn't realised I'd forgotten. Unlike the buzzing of the bees, the human sound was new and unnatural. It was true, I had gotten far too used to nature, as my mother often complained.

Don't swat the wasps! I would hiss in her direction as she darted around. *They're pollinators!*

I am smaller, more colourful in my attire than she is, my hair adorning a flowing scarf decorated with dandelions which I had woven through it, as if the top of my head was a wild field, leaves sprouting in their chosen directions. A bee stops near me often, and I let it hover curiously without flinching. Once it assesses that I am, indeed, a fake flower, the bee flies away, its tiny wings thumping against the plump body.

My body, wingless unlike the bee but heavy nonetheless, now rests on the curved top of a hill. I had fallen asleep in the grass, thoughts and dreams washed away by the rush of a brook. Water flows around an uneven array of large, pointed rocks which shoot out of the waterbed in their excitement to be an inch closer to the sky. They too, had dreams of forming unshakeable mountains, so that neither water nor moss could settle over them. A tiny waterfall, only half a metre in height, trickles beside the rock formation. It sends a pattern of pulses, happy waves tickling the feet of singing frogs who passed the mossy brook on their way to a quieter, darker home sheltered by cattail fences and lily pad roofs.

I lift myself to a seated position now, hearing my mother, far away. As I rise, burying my fingers in damp grass, the frogs look at me nervously before hopping away. Distance distorts my mother's call. I know the sound is my name by pure intuition, even though I cannot pick up the word by ear. I hide my understanding in the brook, pretending that the water had washed away the words, and that I hadn't heard. I want to rest a moment longer, here in my valley where the river flows in perfect sync with the breeze, the same guiding force for the wings of birds and bees alike. The trustworthy wind, when it picks up again, will divert them to a better path than they would have chosen themselves, destiny altering their patterns of flight.

Just as the water shimmers a pale, blue colour, so does the sky, dotted with wispy clouds. I wonder if the birds in the distant sky ever recognise the paths formed by years of human and animal steps between hills and mountains, and the dips of the river which combine to form a portrait of mother nature herself. Could the birds, then, if they let the paths guide their eye, see the tiny flowers whose petals kiss wisps of grass when the wind ties them together? Would they know how the feet of ants pitter-patter against the dirt, how harvest mice rest in pillows of flowerbeds, or the weight of a raindrop on a hummingbird's head? Perhaps better to ask the little lamb, his coat curling around his ears, letting a gust brush wool out of his eyes so that he may admire the stars at night. Does he know that I, too, share the night sky with him, with the bees and the bugs? Does he know of the birds that traverse the horizon, noting him as a white dot among the green valleys?

The same wind that calls them now summons me to return home. There awaits my mother, head tossed with dark, curly hair and questions about my future. In my dreams, her hands trace maps of the mountains in the grass, summoning them at will. Her every breath is powerful enough to generate a tsunami-causing wind, the fluttering eyelashes of her winking eye sending ripples across the water. Raising an arm, she splits the Earth and a crater forms. Men would throw pennies into it, reminding them of forbidden dreams. Between the sea and the endless hills, her love was carried on the dust of vast plains. Where she watered, fruit grew regardless of the season, for if she wished it would be an endless summer. Barrenness, loneliness, these were nightmares only surviving in the depths of a distant ocean, under ever-turbulent waters where rationality was diluted by salt. Smiling, she could predict the future. In my dreams, I grow tall enough to watch the migrating birds, strong enough to hold back my happiness from being swooped up on their travelling feathers. In my dreams to be a woman is to have the world at your fingertips, to feel it as a part of you and calm the trembling earth when it cries. In my dreams we are magnificent women, calling the sun from across the horizon to begin another day.

Letting these thoughts get carried by the passing clouds, I trot back to the house where my mother awaits.

Starving artists

On a cold evening in Galway City, Ireland, buskers' lullabies cradled the evening's shoppers on their path along Shop Street, each passerby sleepy beneath heavy, grey layers of clouds. The damp wind flurried my hair into a tornado-shaped twist, endless humidity forming a perpetual halo of frizz at the crown of my head. Tiny twists and bends in my hair were noticeable only under the faint rays of light. Like soft blankets, the clouds covered the sun, bidding it an early night as it kissed the pointed roofs of Shop Street's dollhouse-like stores and cafes. Each tiny home varied in colour; glistening shades of the rainbow paled by the dewy mist. Their nearly identical, two-storey heights made Galway's main street appear a plaything, innocent and sweet, a toy to people coming from the not-too-distant cities of Dublin and London. Yet this city's charm lay in how easily it was overlooked, the uneven proportion of many buskers to sparse shoppers. The buskers lined the sides of Shop Street, guitars, oboes and vocalists overlapping, while fleeting listeners let the hum recede into background soundtracks for their conversations.

Ireland's art capital is where my story began. I was a young busker in fake leather boots, swaying as the city blurred together in a fog of white. My voice broke a path in the haze for brief moments, showing wandering couples like the burning wicks of candles illuminating a pitch-black room, only for these flickers of light to get caught on a gust and extinguish itself. Attention was hard enough to capture, and money came at even more of a challenge. Buskers didn't earn much. However, I loved the practice to my core. I felt the twisting of intersecting melodies through the background vocals of street chatter. Being on Shop Street, singing, it was like being home. My teeth would crack with a sugar-sweet smile when someone recognised me, stopped and let my singing fill their mind. The best feeling in the world was to be a brief spark, a glistening star. To melt away a stranger's cracked-glass world and show them the true beauty of music. Feelings last forever. Time may pass but we will always have music, bringing men to their knees in tears of drunken love, awakening the insatiable thirst for more feeling. Music takes us by the heart and controls our animal bodies, reshaping our world. With every tequila-soaked defeat I get more pumped to win. I don't just sell music, I breathe music.

Yet most people in my life didn't agree with my inner dialogue. Despite my best efforts to let my love for singing prevail, I wasn't enough of a ditzy daydreamer to avoid financial discussions forever. Soon I would run out of savings and need a stable job, trade my microphone and boots for an apron and serve customers instead of an audience. Lately I faced constant reminders of this inevitable fate. It was easy to live in a daydream before I was jolted awake by my parents calling to ask when I would get a job. It was easy to avoid responsibility before my friends began going on holidays I couldn't afford. I felt trapped at the crossroads in a pitch-black void, unable to see the distance between living out my passion and falling into a debt I couldn't come back from. Every day I woke up wondering when my excitement would be suffocated by the world, asking myself when I would finally shut down and trek down the reasonable path.

The streets darkened as my thoughts did, vibrant colours fading into shadows, engulfed by the mist. Rays of light were disturbed by the fuzzy veil. I squinted my eyes to catch the faint rays of sun settling on a man's outline. He was short and scruffy, an overgrown beard tucked into a mud-splattered leather jacket, eyes bulging from his protruding face as if he couldn't catch a proper breath, face grey and wild like death. His nose was particularly small, and he scratched the sides of it often in discomfort. It was a rare occasion that my own audience could put me off singing, yet I began to feel a growing sense of unease from his lingering stare. It silenced me, a songbird choking in the gaze of an alley cat. I quickly packed up my microphone and its stand into the case I used for transport, hands unsteady in the rush. Adrenaline made them shake as my fingers fumbled with the zipper. Unblinking, the stranger continued to haunt me, stare only broken once when he pushed a phlegmy snort through his throat and sinuses, making him cough and close the predating eyes. Had he gotten closer? I turned my back to him, too afraid to see if he was coming closer. I imagined his hot breath drenched in tobacco, dust from his hands pouring over me and drowning me until I ceased to exist. The frightening vision pushed me to walk in the wrong direction, letting narrow alleyways guide me through a longer route home, safe from his view. Grey, tiled paths enveloped me, darkness providing refuge. Yet I could hear steps ripping through the plastic illusion of safety, my dollhouse world being ripped apart. I picked up the pace. His breath was violent with fatigue from the chase, pants interchanging with gaps leaving the bearded mouth. My clicking heels rang like cowbells attached to my feet, the sound of prey rushing away to hide its scent from the tiger. Nothing was fast enough. I was moving slower than a slug entangled in a cocoon, hearing my steps patter faster, yet feeling my body push through the streets more and more slowly. I turned a corner at a snail's pace, my heartbeat so loud that I could no longer identify the breaths and footsteps. It was the heartbeat of a doll whose cottage's roof had been ripped off, watching a giant's hand reach to grab her matted hair.

"Hello!"

I froze, the sound of steps seemingly continuing without me. In a dreamlike state, I stood still, looking up at the muddy sky and down at my leather boots. The heavy footsteps were mine all along. Returning to my body, I staggered at the weight of my lungs. The heavy breaths had been mine as well. Hot on my trail had been my own panting mouth, the danger non-existent. Yet the voice, had the voice too been an illusion? I flung my head around, hunting for the sight of the heeled doll.

"Hello!" Echoed the doll's voice again. It was a high-pitched, soft voice deepened by an unfriendly maturity, as if the doll herself was trying to frighten me. There was something unreal to it, and I would have been content believing that she was a figment of a fatigue-driven imagination, had a gust of wind not carried her rose-scented hair into my cheek.

"Hello," she repeated. Above me hung the silhouette of a distinguished woman, her long limbs stretched out like an elegant tower. She wore a crown tucked carefully into her spiked, blonde hair which reflected light of unknown origin. Her glowing frame was tall and sharp-edged, nails and crown sticking up into the air like the crisp New York City skyline. Every initial observation told me to marvel at her, that the world demanded attention for this woman. She was adorned with a pale, pink dress, starting with thin, shoulder straps and blossoming into layers of tulle, creating a wide, almost ethereal silhouette. Her eyes were those of a curious cat, decorated messily with sparkling eyeshadow and smudged eyeliner, most likely drawn with fumbling hands in a morning rush. It made her relatable, unlike the rest of her perfectly layered makeup, it showed me that even her uncracked face could have flaws. Glistening teeth may have hidden in her smile, wide and dangerous like a shark, yet I could also see that the red pigment was smudged around the crown of her lip. In a flash, her voice was close and real, mouth inches away from my ear. Blonde streaks ran down my shoulders as she hugged me intimately, pushing her fingers into my waist and then immediately letting go.

"It's a pleasure to finally meet you." Her smile remained unchanged except for her eyes, which flickered between predator and ally as she sized me up.

"Hello." I straightened, trying to match her height. She must have been close to two metres tall.

"My name, dear, is Miss Knightin Amour. You may address me as such." Despite her regular voice sounding faintly Irish, she enunciated each syllable in her name with a distinct French accent, gurgling the elongated word *amour* in the back of her throat.

"Hello, Miss Amour."

"Have you, by chance, considered…" she leaned in seductively and whispered the next words into my ear, her hot breath dizzying me. She smelt of flowers and sweat.

"No," I stammered, dazed.

""Oh, well that's a shame then. I think we'd make it worth your while," she laughed, cackle bouncing off the roofs of houses. I felt her presence grow far above them now, like she was the greatest force in this city, shoulders strong and legs ready to chase me if I ran, even in her pair of platform heels.

"I'm not so sure about that," I pronounced slowly. My body was frozen in place as she wrapped her smooth arm around me. I was a mouse caught in the trap of a beautiful snake. She squeezed my arm suddenly, and I jumped with a frightened inhale.

"Don't be spooked, dear! My, my, you're so cold. What's wrong with having a talent agent now anyway? Look, I promise I'm not some kind of scammer. I heard you sing, and you're pretty good. We could work something out together, make it all professional. We're a proper agency for rising stars in Galway, if you just let me take you to the studio and show you around then you'll see what we're all about."

I stood silently, not knowing what to say.

She continued, "you know, we've got lots of local talent represented already. We could make a pretty penny together, get you some backup dancers and a guitarist! Just imagine performing all around the country, and not just in church choirs. People lining up to see you, an array of backup dancers flinging their hot bodies behind you. What a rush! And, of course, all that ticket revenue would be yours after a fee. We're very fair with our prices."

"No, thank you Miss." I turned and took a few steps in a random direction before she called out after me.

"Come on now! Do you know how hard it is to make a living as a musician alone?"

I thought for a moment, my confidence increasing. "If I'm good enough for you to chase me down the street, surely I'm good enough to make it on my own?" I turned, staring deeply into Miss Amour's eyes, watching her confidence diminish under my gaze.

I continued, "you take commission for everything my music earns right? Isn't that how it works? So, naturally you'll pick someone who'll be a cash cow, stuck in a contract that stops benefitting me in a year. No thank you, I don't want to be locked in anyone's cage."

"Aw, that's not true now." To my surprise, she sat down in the street, her layered dress fluttering. She lay the points of her shoes parallel to the pavement and stretched her long legs. "You know, it's tough to be in this industry. The least you could do is hear me out, for the sake of sisterhood, right? How about a bit of camaraderie, eh? I ran all this way, didn't I?"

Something about her little whine, the way that I had humbled this woman, ignited faint guilt within me. After all, we were both artists trying to make a living. With all my financial fears, with all my worries of losing my freedom, perhaps taking a gamble was worth it.

"I suppose you did come all this way," I drawled. "Just a short meeting is alright."

"Right!" She jumped up, landing perfectly. "That's settled then!"

With no warning, Miss Amour grew tall and vibrant again, resting her pink press-on nails against my knuckles as her strong hand slid into mine. She pulled me, strong like a horse, and I fought for my balance as she trotted down the street quickly. The heavy footsteps and clicking heels from earlier made only one sound now, perfectly pitched steps in unison.

The walk was dizzying. I counted four left turns and no rights, meaning that we should have ended up exactly where we started. This, however, was not the case. The bustling stores and crowds were gone, and Shop Street's bustle couldn't even be heard. The sun was still out, it wasn't possible that the city had fallen asleep already. Yet as I stood in front of the empty residences, Galway had become desolate and lonely. Every window was barricaded in some way, either with curtains or an absence of light. Lost and having no other person to rely on, I deepened my grasp of Miss Amour's hand, noticing a meek expression on her face. She looked confident that I would accept whatever was proposed now. I asked myself whether I would, and before my subconscious had a moment to shake an answer to the surface, my thoughts were interrupted.

"Down we go, love."

I followed her down a small staircase into a basement entrance behind a two-storey, white residential building. Moss and mildew lined the door and keyhole, which Miss Amour fiddled with for a while before managing to turn the key successfully. The door opened with a ghostly creak, revealing only darkness. We entered. I felt myself tumble through hallway after hallway, tunnels wide and dark, Miss Amour glistening like a flashlight as she led me further through the cave-like property. Finally, we arrived, which I would not have noticed if not for Miss Amour's sudden halt. The room was still entirely dark, and I could not make out anything resembling a recording studio. As far as I was aware, we were the only two people in the room.

"Love, welcome to the Queens Studio of Galway. Best talent agency in town for stars of different paths, representing only the brightest," she announced, as if reading a telemarketer's speech.

An array of golden light bulbs spelt out the words *QUEENS STUDIO*, taking their time to flicker before turning on completely, flooding my eyes with harsh light. I took a step back, blinded. I hadn't managed to take a proper look around the studio, the only things illuminated were Miss Amour, and another person's distant silhouette. The room appeared endless and vast, and I was so desperately drawn to the idea of opportunity hidden behind the lights, imagining a professional set up, a floating microphone behind glass walls. Miss Amour would sit in the producer's seat and remix the beat I sang to, her long nails tapping away at a variety of flickering buttons and knobs on an enormous screen. My eyes searched through the dark for glasses full of champagne and a red carpet, instead settling on a man's approaching figure.

"Allow me to introduce my partner in crime, Harrison."

As Miss Amour introduced him, Harrison came closer. The two partners could not have differed more. While Miss Amour stared at me like a cat circling dinner, eyes catching the faint light like a watchful crow predicting my next move, Harrison's presence was that of a ghost. His thick eyebrows shielded his deep-set eyes from the glow, making the eyes concave into the face. Even as he stepped closer, I couldn't imagine I was looking at a human, darkness pooling in his face. I retreated but my back hit an icy wall, the cold brick drawing goosebumps up my arms. The hair on the back of my neck stretched up towards the exit, even towards the empty street. I began to hope that something else could be out there for me.

"Hi, Harrison, it's nice to meet you." I couldn't say no. It was sufficiently frightening to be trapped in an unknown basement with two strangers, knowing that either of them could overpower me if they needed to, without having an air of tension to cause me more anxiety. I trembled with fear, trying not to cause any issues and put myself in an irreversible situation. My blood pumping against my sweaty skin, I let myself detach from the wall and shake Harrison's hairy hand with as much politeness as I could muster.

"Could we turn the lights on, please?" I tried to stabilise my quivering voice.

"Oh, honey," Harrison cackled, Miss Amour distantly joining with a laugh. "Is this not bright enough for you? Looks like we've got a proper star on our hands!"

"No, really, I feel a bit unwell." I raised a weak arm above my head, letting it block some light from my eyes. "Just, regular light please. If it's not too much trouble, I'm a bit overwhelmed."

Neither of them moved to turn a light on. Instead, deep and booming like a priest showing me the way to a church confessional, Harrison asked me a question.

"What brought you here? What's really overwhelming you?"

I hadn't expected this. Maybe it was caused by the lack of light, the fatigue, the dizzying walk, or a divine force stronger than I was, but I suddenly loosened my shoulders and let the darkness eat my inner thoughts. My mouth ran faster than my brain, wild and free, my recent stress flowing out of me as smoothly as an ocean's waves against the shoreline. In the darkness I gave two strangers, who I should have been running away from, the key to my soul.

"It's so easy to be good once." I began. "Everyone applauds you once, you remember it forever. It's a great moment, really. Then you wake up the next morning and nothing changes. You don't feel any smarter, any more experienced, but suddenly you're carrying a monkey on your back and that monkey comes with you to every social event, and every family dinner, and it screams in your ear when you're trying to sleep. It keeps asking when you'll do more. When you'll beat your own record. Everyone's standards are high – but your own are the worst. Suddenly performing is exhausting and nothing you do is good enough. Learning, trying, it loses all value. Suddenly I have to make money and move to a new city to chase a dream I didn't realise I had. Suddenly I'm not a silly highschooler who won a talent show, instead I'm a failed prodigy and I can't blame anyone except myself.

Most days I wish I wasn't good at all, because living with the pressure of making money from my talent is just unbearable."

I stopped to breathe. Without saying a word, Miss Amour turned the overhead lights on. She was sitting on a laundry machine, leaning sideways so her crown didn't pierce a washing line dotted with bras and men's underwear. I understood now that Miss Amour and Harrison's studio was only real in the darkness, in a place where dreams held more power than reality. Why she had been so heartbroken when I initially rejected her. I was no cash cow for a greedy business. Rather, before me were two struggling artists who thought I might have the potential to save them.

"Yeah, love. I know," Miss Amour whispered, teary-eyed. "I know."

Standing in the mouldy basement, heels resting on the cracked floor, Miss Amour's wig no longer shone. Without a film of mystery over her, I could now notice the spots where makeup dribbled down her face from the sweat pooling under many layers of foundation. With the makeup mask slipping off her skin, I truly saw the real person inside. Not predation, but desperation had asked her to hunt me in the streets of

Galway. Two dolls with messy lives, in the basement of a house that fate's jittering hands had thrown us into, we came to a small understanding. I turned to Harrison, giving a silent nod to let him speak.

"We're struggling, kid. Guess you saw right through us."

Letting go of the beast I'd imagined before, Harrison's true face formed in front of me. I understood now. The matted red beard and jacket, darkened with the stains of half-reached dreams. The man who had been staring earlier, not out of violence and hate, but rather stuck watching me live out an echo of his own past. His bulging eyes were curious and afraid, and the bloated face pushed his cheeks into a deeper smile. I had been so, so wrong.

"I saw you earlier," I whispered.

"I noticed that."

"Does that happen often?"

"I'm not much of a looker," he replied, not unhappily. "Didn't mean to frighten you."

"I know that now."

Meanwhile, Miss Amour was removing her makeup with a damp wipe, perched up on a buzzing laundry machine. She kicked off her heels to reveal blistered, blue feet, too large to be stuffed into the shoes without pain. Her toes spread out in the air, yellow nails cracked and fragmenting. I watched her carefully push the wipe around her eyes and lips, shrinking again in front of me as her overlined makeup dissolved. Stubble peered out from patches on and around her chin. Her wig dropped to the ground, revealing a smooth, bald head.

"Bradley was our first star," Harrison explained. "We came up with a look, a name, for the drag persona. Knightin Amour. It was perfect, the brand, the look. We were going to be social media famous; we'd read every book and followed every online guide. Spent all our money on courses, we did. Didn't earn a thing. That's how life goes sometimes, eh?"

Miss Amour, now undressing to change into the identity of Bradley, sighed.

"Hey, we had a good time doing it all, didn't we?"

"Was it worth it?" I asked, sobered by what I'd seen before me. I saw not Miss Amour, tall and glamorous, but rather Bradley, young and poor, voice buzzing from the roll of the laundry machine beneath. My world began to crack, the plastic walls of my dollhouse life melting under the burning light of reality. I thought of all the talents, all the hardworking artists that the world would never hear of, and of all the authors and painters who didn't become famous until long after their deaths. What was all of it for, if my life would be harsh and brutal, face bruised from falling again and again into failure's arms? I realised now why I had taken this meeting in the first place, why I was still here despite the fear and panic I had felt initially. I needed to know what to do next. I needed to know whether to return my mother's calls and receive a reality check or continue holding onto my dream.

Before hearing their response, I wanted to stop the conversation and scream out. I didn't want my illusion to be broken, my connection to the crowds severed. I still wanted to live in my false reality, be a hungry artist on the streets of Galway, singing under the mist and hearing the clink of pennies thrown into the hats of dozens of others just like me. I wanted to clasp my hands over my ears and dart away, into the street where my dreams were still alive. Yet I didn't. I waited for what Bradley and Harrison had to say.

Instead, I got a response that suited me just fine.

"Worth it?" Bradley cackled, Miss Amour still burning inside. "Oh, beyond worth it!"

Harrison let out a grin too. "Yeah, kid. Don't be fooled by our little sappy moment there. We're gonna keep fighting for this. The real question is, are you with us?"

Day at the zoo

By all conventional, human metrics, the mother baboon is not a beautiful creature. When she walks, her red bottom jerks through the air like a deformed *STOP* sign, kinks and knots displayed for all around to wince at. Twenty metres in the air, she can squash her ass onto a tree perch, and chunks of it still hang off. The pieces of flesh wag in the wind, tauntingly. Pieces of hay stick out of her fur wildly, and mud and bark are stuck under her claws from a lifetime of digging and climbing around her enclosure. Her body is bulbous, and she has a large face with an unreadable expression. Despite appearing closer to a human than many other animals, her form is ridiculed instead of related to.

Continuing to use human metrics, the mother baboon is not a friendly creature either. Her coat of hair is not in reach for people to stroke and pat, like a cat, dog, or guinea pig. They do not imagine it to be soft and wispy, as they know that the mother baboon would bare her teeth and roar, attacking as soon as she is touched. She does not smile, and when she makes a face resembling a smile, it is one of anger. Oftentimes this is because her children are fighting, or she feels threatened. Except for these moments, she sits with a neutral, almost bored expression. Up on her tree perch, she is a distant, unrelatable animal. She looks out across the horizon and no one else knows what she sees.

Because humans do not perceive beauty or domesticable characteristics in the mother baboon, they will laugh and point at her. They stare, despite not wanting to, unable to divert their eyes from her flashing, red bottom. Children, especially, poke and prod their parents with questions.

"What's wrong with his butt?" Comes the call of a young one.

"I wonder why they evolved that way. Like, what's the benefit of that?" Even teenagers are impressed.

The mother baboon does not understand this human mockery. In fact, she does not attach much value to the sounds of humans, unless, of course, they're paired with the smell of supper. The only sounds which regularly turn the head of the mother baboon are the hungry cries of her many youths. They call for her, twiddling their fingers towards the sky to assess if there is a teat directly above, to be stuffed into their mouth for a ready supply of milk. The long, pink teats sway and shake as she climbs towards her babies.

Their eyes are closed and content as they feed. That is the only important sight to the mother baboon, and it is one she encounters regularly.

She does not see her own reflection, seldom for humid days after heavy spring rain. On those particular days, when it is not hot enough for the rainwater to evaporate nor cold enough for it to freeze, translucent puddles form at the bottom of her dusty enclosure. If the puddle is positioned in a clean spot, and it has not been run through many times by the trampling feet of the wild youths, the mother may witness a hairy baboon in the water. Her fur shakes as she edges her head to look more closely, and the baboon in the puddle does too, its face tilting in unison. It has a mouth crammed with teeth, and expressionless eyes. The mother baboon continues to evaluate the baboon in the puddle. When she sees the teats of the baboon in the puddle, she recognises a fellow mother, and at once decides that her reflection is more friend than foe. Accepting the fellow baboon, she continues with her day. No more thoughts, no more pondering. The puddle, after a few quiet minutes, is jumped into by a group of babies, the water turning dark and opaque from showers of dust thrown into the water by the young apes. It will be a long time before the mother baboon's next encounter with her reflection.

Across the enclosure, two baboons watch a plastic pacifier fall into the enclosure after being dropped by a human child. They fight over it violently, swinging on the tail of a teenage baboon who has grasped the plastic in its mouth and attempts to climb a tree to get away from her siblings. The teenage baboon falls to the ground, catching herself with her springy legs, but the pacifier has slipped from her lips and been taken away by another. Defeated and tired, she climbs to the top stump of her tree. From here she can admire the full scene, her mother yanking the youngest baboon for mealtime, the rest scampering to be next, climbing over and pushing each other. The teenage baboon also sees the human child who had dropped the plastic object. The human child reaches for its mother, five fingers on a shaking hand, trying to demonstrate that it has lost its precious item. The teenage baboon turns to see her siblings, their five-fingered baboon hands touching the mother's fur. It seems that the human child, too, had baboon hands. From this height, the human child appears just as far away as her own siblings did. She will never jump, however. Her instinct always stops her.

Today the teenage baboon watches humans disappear into the distance, hands just like hers, and then climbs to join her family, decorated ass shown to the whole world. After some years, she too might greet the mother monkey in the puddle with a knowing look.

Lean on me

Vague chatter blurred into the background; true coherence of thought left behind as the train pulled out of the station. Its engine sped up, whistling a lonely tune. For most of the journey, more sheep than people would bear witness to this chain of metal wagons being pulled across the Danish countryside. The trip from Copenhagen to Esbjerg took passengers across the entire landscape of the country, directly from the east to west coast of the Danish mainland.

A passenger inside the train was Jackie, an American woman living in Copenhagen for the last few months. She was on a work assignment for her tech job, learning from Denmark's innovation hub and hoping to gather skills to earn her a promotion back home. Yet now, as she shifted in her seat in discomfort, she didn't feel like a top performer in her field. She was stuck in a strange situation, rather unsure of the appropriate manners to use.

The man sitting beside Jackie had fallen asleep, his head inching closer to her shoulder at an alarming rate, instead of towards the window where it belonged. At this rate, Jackie felt she had only minutes until his body slumped into hers. She didn't want to be touched by a stranger. The window was quite clearly the man's personal space, and so, naturally, the space between the seats must belong to Jackie. It was only fair to divide the train up in this manner. Had this encounter began between stops which were close together, she could have politely awoken him with a tap on the shoulder, feigning worry that he would miss a stop and travel too far. This would both free her from the potential of turning into his personal travel pillow and make him perceive her as a kind and sensible person. It would have been perfect. If she was very lucky, she might have done this just before the stop he was to get off at, which would save him from missing it. She could have been a hero!

However, the man's eyes had shut before the train had even left. Like a tiny baby tucked into a pram on an autumn walk, the vehicle's movement lulled him into a deep sleep. There was no opportunity to be a hero, nor free herself. She was at the mercy of this stranger's bobbing head, almost at rest on her shoulder now.

Jackie, lost in thought, collected herself enough to become aware of herself staring. Unembarrassed, for really it was his fault for leaning so close into her personal space, she took the opportunity to notice his physical features. He had straight, thick, red hair and pale skin kissed with freckles up and down his exposed arms, neck and face. The rest could be left to the imagination. Jackie blushed at the thought, raising her hand unknowingly to feel the warmth of her maroon face. In doing so, she startled the man awake.

"Oh, sorry about that," he chuckled, straightening his posture. He had a thick accent, though Jackie was not adapted enough to distinguish which part of Denmark it could be from. She'd been told that if it sounded closer to Swedish, the accent was from the east. If it sounded more German, it was from the south-west. Jackie took a mental note of this, despite not knowing what either Swedish or German sounded like.

"No worries." She lowered her face until her gaze was firmly planted on the aisle's floor.

She felt him turn away too, then sigh deeply into the empty fields. Jackie looked out of the window. The train sped by, the view melting together into waves of green. Sometimes a lighter shade stood out, sometimes a darker one, but always green.

"Where are you off to then?" He asked, not turning back.

Jackie thought for a moment before replying.

"Last stop."

"Esbjerg?" Somehow, he knew how to dig for the information.

She didn't want to tell him. She hadn't told anyone back home, and she didn't want to look back on her life decisions as being guided by a stranger. Jackie had always been prone to people pleasing, breaking herself when faced with the criticism of others. Everyone who met her told her that she was a pushover, an anxious mess who couldn't make her own decisions. If this stranger asked nicely enough, maybe she could have been convinced to get off at Esbjerg, or another stop, and stay there. She didn't belong anywhere, anyway.

"Ah," he smacked his lips in satisfaction, "it seems the myths have reached foreigners too."

"I live here, actually."

"Yes, but you're not from here, are you? I'd guess…" he pondered a while, and Jackie in the meanwhile found herself tilting towards him with no warning.

Her body was behaving independently of her conscious mind.

"Manhattan. New York," she stammered, wondering how much he knew of American geography, "the States, the American States."

Jackie took a deep inhale before gathering her words.

"I'm from the United States of America," she announced like a TV show host.

"Yes, I know where New York is," he chuckled, over-pronouncing the letter *o* in *York*, dragging it out so it lasted longer than the rest of the sentence. "So, why the last stop then? If you're from the land of dreams."

"That's not something to discuss with a stranger."

"I'm Lasse. Lasse from Gribskov."

They shook hands.

"Gribskov. Skov, like forest," Jackie thought aloud.

"Nice. She speaks some Danish."

"Not a lot, not a lot. I moved to Copenhagen recently, so I've been taking the free classes."

"Why are you here, Jackie?"

She was caught off-guard again. "I work for a tech company. It's part of a collaborative project between

North America and Europe. I was sent here to share best practices from different firms by collecting and compiling various reports from programmers, both here and back home."

The word *home* sounded strange in her mouth. Leaving had not made her homesick whatsoever, even though she had so terribly wished that it would. She wanted to miss her friends, run up to her family with open arms in the airport. Yet as she thought about her return, prepared to go back to her life, she felt only emptiness. Having moved to New York straight after college, separated from her friends and family for years, she'd made little effort to keep in contact. Everything was about working harder, working faster, fuelling her ambition. Now she felt worn from the stress of her job, and the cold, lonely, single life she'd created for herself.

"What do you want from the last stop?" Lasse asked, as if reading her mind.

"You first," she huffed.

"I'm not taking the train all the way. I'm getting off at Roskilde."

"I don't believe that." Jackie was shocked at her own assertiveness. "You know all about the last stop, and no one would be able to resist it if they knew. No regular person would miss the opportunity to go back in time, to change their life's trajectory."

Lasse smirked in response. "Guess I'm not regular then."

Jackie leaned back into her seat, exasperated. Seeing her surprise, Lasse continued. His tone was friendly, with a hint of teasing.

"You really think people are that unhappy? Sure, maybe a myth about a time-travelling train, which supposedly takes you back to your greatest mistake after the Esbjerg stop, will get a couple of people talking. Probably not those who live on the coast though, they'd be afraid of dropping right into the water if the train kept going. It's not like Esbjerg's a port city or anything, right?" He took a moment to laugh at his own joke before continuing. "I doubt people even believe in it. Those who are gullible, who consider that it could be true, do you really think they'd just give up everything that they've worked so hard for, the lives they've built? Why would they bother?"

"I'm gullible, huh?"

"That's not what I am saying."

"I think hindsight is everything. If you know that your life could be better, why not do it?"

"I don't believe in a quick fix. Life is long and beautiful."

"Then get off the train," Jackie said sternly. She traced her hand down to her backpack below her seat, rummaging in it for a book to read. Anything to occupy her mind. Instead, the person pulling out an object was Lasse.

His train ticket glimmered in front of Jackie's eyes. *Copenhagen to Roskilde.* A one-way ticket for a small city coming up soon, not anywhere close to Esbjerg.

The train halted. Jackie didn't know what stop they were at, where in Denmark she was. All she could see was the light reflecting off the ticket, and the destination *Roskilde* spelt out in English letters. The Danish name was the exact same. The number of zones he was travelling was highlighted underneath.

Her own ticket said *Esbjerg*, though her hopes were to stay on the train and experience the legend. She needed it to be real. How could he not believe in it? Why would he mock her?

"Great. So now you get to laugh at me. Go ahead." Anger was hot on the tip of her tongue.

"Why are you unhappy, Jackie?"

The train departed once more, yet Lasse's silhouette was perfectly still against the moving blur of endless green. His eyes were stuck onto hers, staring deeply.

"You don't even believe in it. Stop making fun of me." She didn't know how to turn away. Her eyes had lost all connection with the movements of her body, they were a stranger's now.

"I do believe in it. I just don't care. I don't want to change my life."

"You really wouldn't try it out?" she whispered, stunned by this response.

"Nope," he said cheerily.

"You're not curious?"

"Nope."

"Not even a little?"

"Not even a little."

Jackie had only one question left to ask.

"Why?"

Lasse replied slowly, "I don't believe in any perfect choice, or even any correct choice. You get what you get. I think everything I've been through, everything I live with, it taught me something. It made me stronger, braver. There is no perfect life Jackie, it's not possible.

Maybe you'll go back in time and get rich, and then you can be equally miserable surrounded by cash. Or whatever your dream is. You fulfil it, but you don't fulfil yourself. Take some time off, go for a walk, see a museum and think of all the people before you that tried a quick fix for their issues and found out it didn't make a difference. There's a good Viking Museum in Roskilde, by the way."

"Is that why you're going to Roskilde?"

"No, I have some business there. My family." Lasse looked out of the window for a dazed moment, then snapped back into the conversation when Jackie replied.

"I see. Regardless, I don't think I agree. I've spent so much time worried, anxious, making myself sick. Wasting my life."

"So, get off the train and stop reminiscing about the past. Change the future."

"No." Jackie decided.

"Alright then." Lasse mumbled. "You know, the one regret I probably do have is not spending more time appreciating my family. My friends, my wife. Work, it comes and goes. It's always there, someone always wants you to work. People, though, they won't always ask for your love. You have to remember to give it to them." Jackie looked to him as someone, despite him being young and them only recently meeting, who was rather set in his principles. He reminded her of her ex-partner, Ben, who she missed terribly. They'd made the decision to split only a week into her moving away. She'd told him that it would be too much effort, that they both needed to focus on their careers.

If you love something, let it go. True love will find you again.

But what's the point? What if you let go one too many times and realise that you don't know how to hold on anymore? How much letting go is enough? As she wondered, she drifted to a soft sleep.

In her dreams, Jackie stood by a cycle lane in downtown Copenhagen, holding her breath and fearing the crossing. It was a late summer's day during her first week in Copenhagen. This was a memory deeply painful for her. It was a reminder of her indecisiveness, of the way she constantly put herself into uncomfortable situations to avoid any sort of pain or change. Even excitement and learning were deemed too risky. She strayed away from the new.

To an untrained eye Copenhagen's bike lane
bonanza might appear similar to the motorcycle-
clogged roads of Vietnam. Yet, as Jackie had found out
in the recent weeks, the two could not differ more.
After being yelled at by many bikers, she realised she
could not walk smoothly across the bicycle lanes here
in hope that the experienced bikers would knowingly
dodge her. Copenhagen's law-loving citizens could not
handle the horrors of having a pedestrian walk across
the lane if they were within four metres distance, and
so she got accustomed to hearing bike bells ring
whenever she tried to get across the road.

One, two. The bikes swooshed past her rapidly.
Mothers comfortably wheeled multiple children in
wagons at the front of bicycles, barely breaking a
sweat. Some wore helmets and long, tight shorts,
racing by and taking their eyes off the road only for
brief seconds to check their exercise watches. Children
swivelled and swung themselves around, learning to
cycle before they could walk. Jackie didn't feel ready.

This wasn't the first time that Copenhagen
managed to dizzy her with a new sound, smell, or
habit. She had not yet gotten used to the Danish
language, she had only English and vague Spanish

phrases in her back pocket. Beyond the language barrier, which was expected, she had seemingly thousands of cultural aspects to get used to. No one blessed her when she sneezed. No one tried to make small talk at the bus stop. No one stopped when she tried to cross the cycle lane. Perhaps all of these were silly trivialities for the citizens of a tiny, flat country with better health coverage than the majority of the world, where people got paid by the government to attend university, but these little things made everything seem wild and unknown to Jackie. It was all more than she had expected, more than she could take. The first time that she truly felt meaningless.

In her memory, she didn't cross. Instead, she turned back and took the first train to her dorm, where she'd cried, and cried. She didn't call anyone, didn't search for a connection. Jackie had let herself be swept up by a loss of self-importance, the wave morphing into a loss of self-confidence as it crashed on the shore, and finally receding back into an ocean of low self-worth. Never in her mind could she have thought that this strange, little memory was definitive in shaping her experience. Most days she didn't remember her first week, let alone an unimportant day where she had nothing to do and nowhere to be.

Thoughtful, she sat on the grass beside the bike lane, noticing the bikes sweep past her in waves. There was no sign of the right choice, no guideline for how to behave. She crossed her legs and let the spikes of grass pinch her, tickling and scraping her bare legs. It was a hot summer's day, and she didn't have anywhere in particular to be. She let herself watch the bike wheels turning onwards, and onwards, again and again, people leaning on the handrails and breathing heavily against the occasional wind. Everyone here had somewhere to be. It occurred to her then, that she was lonely. She picked up her phone mindlessly, dialling a number she remembered by heart.

"Hey, Jacks," came the familiar mumble, his voice gritty, throat hoarse with sleep.

"Hi, did I wake you?"

"No, no." He was obviously lying. "I was just getting ready for hockey."

A late afternoon in Denmark was still the early morning in New York. Ben must have been awoken by the sound of the phone ringing. Jackie slapped herself on the forehead, quietly, and felt the embarrassment scrape at her.

"You shouldn't sleep with your phone on! All your notifications would wake you up!"

"Did you call me just to yell at me?" He sounded like he was smiling.

"No, I'm sorry," she whispered lovingly. "I miss you. Things are… different here."

"Different, how?"

"I feel unimportant somehow. All the time. I used to feel so big, so grand, like I could do anything. This place is meant to be so much smaller, I thought I'd be…"

"Even bigger? Gosh, Jacks, maybe there's no room," he laughed.

"Well, that's not what I meant!" Jackie whined. "No one here thinks I'm interesting, or cool, or anything. It's like, what's the point of doing this anyway?"

Ben let out another chuckle.

"You don't get what I mean."

"Where are you right now?"

Jackie flushed. "I'm sitting by a bike lane, in the grass. It was hard to cross so I just wanted to take a minute, talk to you, feel normal maybe."

"Is the neighbourhood nice?"

"It's so pristine. So clean. Makes me miss New York."

"Really? New York is so… lived in. That's putting it nicely, I guess."

"I like that it's lived in. I didn't think so then, but I do now. Everything is too pretty, too perfect here. Back home it felt like everyone around had something in common, like we shared something. You saw a mural and you knew it was painted by someone who moved here to pursue a dream. Probably someone young. Here there's no graffiti, no nothing. Everything looks brand new and shiny, like it's made of glass."

"Wow."

"You sound tired. Should I stop?"

"No, no." Ben yawned. "Keep going."

"Technically, the city is old. So it's probably me that's the issue. I just feel like imperfections are covered up here somehow. I keep worrying they'll cover me up."

"Like, they'll kill you?"

"No!" she squeaked anxiously before realising the joke. "More like, that I don't belong. I felt that way back home too, though. Everything is hard. I make it hard. I'm sorry for calling, anyway. It was silly."

"Life is hard, Jacks."

"I know, I know. I should just suck it up."

"No, love. Life is hard. Let me be there for you. Let me support you. I know you feel unimportant. Everything is new, everything is difficult. But isn't it nice to be unimportant for once, too? No one relies on you, no one's chasing you. You just get to exist, do something fun. No one needs you to be the most talented or the most hardworking. Sounds like you don't have to fight to survive anymore."

Jackie exhaled slowly. The summer air was warm and clean. The breath muffled the sound of the bikes, the dinging bells and the skidding wheels against the pavement.

"You're right. Thank you."

"I love you. Talk soon."

"I love you."

Picking herself up, she let her frame stand tall against the bikers. Her feet rested in the soil for a moment before she let her heartbeat fall into an even pattern, breathing naturally. Jackie took a step onto the path, into the unknown. Eyes wide open and hands unclenched, she let herself push against the flow, finding her own space amidst the never-ending rhythm of bikes. She marvelled at how they parted for her, how no one yelled. She hadn't gotten in anyone's way, she hadn't disrupted the traffic whatsoever. Unknown to her, there had always been a space for someone walking just a little differently. All she had needed was to take a step onto the path.

The train started to slow down. Jackie was awake, finding herself leaning on Lasse's shoulder. She lifted herself slowly, the dream having distorted her perceptions. Leaning on someone had awoken something in her. She rubbed her eyes sleepily.

"You stayed on," she uttered. "You didn't get off at Roskilde."

Lasse turned to her, raising an eyebrow.

"Roskilde is the next stop, actually."

Jackie sat up with a startled jolt. Adrenaline rushed through her body.

"Wait." Her head shook, looking around the train, "we didn't get there? But..."

Lasse looked at her in concern, without a clue as to what she meant or why she was so excited. Jackie began to pack her things urgently.

"How far until Roskilde?" she asked.

"Couple of minutes. Why?"

"I have to get off and go back to Copenhagen." Jackie's eyes exploded with firework tears. "I have to catch a flight."

She stepped off the train, hands clasped tightly around the handles of her backpack. Jackie found the platform which should have contained her train back home but found it empty. Lasse had disappeared down a dark street of the city, and not a single other person was around now. The only other voice was that of a train announcer.

"Dear passengers. We are experiencing serious delays around Valby Station. There will be no trains from Roskilde to Copenhagen at this time. Thank you for your patience."

Jackie was trapped here. Unable to get home, to continue living her newfound dream of connecting with the past, she found the energy rush inside her unbearable. She needed action. Adrenaline pushed her further, faster, walking down a street into the city of Roskilde. She picked a street at random, turning back once to see if the train station had come back to life behind her. It had not. No trains entered or departed.

"So, this is how we part ways," she said to the station, decisively pushing forward. "Thank you, stranger."

Roskilde's tiny homes were vibrant despite the night's desperate attempts to hide their colour. A one-storey residence glistened a pale blue with freshly painted, white window frames, like a faint reminder of the daytime sky. Most houses were short, colourful stumps poking out from the old roads, cobblestone making the wheels of cars jump. Only a few cars passed, and otherwise the city displayed few signs of life. The trees loomed, their long shadows chasing Jackie down the path, but she outpaced them.

She could not stop her feet from moving. Her head rushed with blood, pounding, as she dazed past an enormous cathedral. It was spotlighted, orange lights making it stand out in the town, one of the few things visible as Jackie walked beyond the steady streets and further into untouched wilderness. The sharp points of the cathedral's roof pierced the void of the sky, fighting the heavy dark, but when Jackie turned away, she found herself entirely lost. The darkness grew in intensity. Jackie found her body wading through deep grass, pacing into a huge park like a lost ghost.

The trees here could touch the sky, far taller than those before. They swayed, enormous leaves raining down and throwing Jackie's frail body into the depths.

Her mouth filled with tasteless dirt. Suddenly, Roskilde's soil opened, and she sank, like a tiny grain in a deep silo. Jackie screamed, and screamed, but the only consequence was the filling of her lungs with sand until they weighed too much to force a cough. Further into the Earth's core she sank, helpless and silent.

Finally, she could see again. Jackie now sat on a soft patch of grass. No dirt, no grain of sand clung to her, and her lungs were filled only with fresh, clean air. She took a long breath, letting her stomach expand like a balloon, chest expanding and rising. Once she confirmed that she could breathe, she checked her heart. It beat evenly, thumps reverberating through her body gently. The panic and anxiety from before were gone, cleared from the body. Now, Jackie was ready to look around.

On a small hill, grass tickled her ankles just as they did when she struggled to cross the bike lane. Now, however, she sat before an oasis of unfathomable beauty. Tracing her gaze down the hill, Jackie saw a small marsh, home to frogs and tiny turtles. Spotted toads splashed water onto each other with their large hops, slimy bodies wobbling and shaking. Dragonflies zapped across a large lake near the marsh, stopping at random increments to hover and vibrate their powerful, humming wings, as if unsure where to go next. They hovered just above the water's surface, clear and turquoise to reflect the green shrubs and blue sky. She heard birds singing their throats raw in the background, overjoyed to be alive in a natural haven. The lake circled a small island with one, single, large tree erected from it. It bore neither flowers nor leaves, yet it grew long, thick sticks in a variety of directions like the needle spikes of a hedgehog. Surrounding the oasis was a dense layer of bush, such that no view of the outside was possible. The only way out was up, a direction which the birds and flies took but Jackie could not. She looked to the pale, blue sky. The sun hid behind the tall bushes, yet there was no shortage of daylight. Everything was vibrant in her vision.

She rose, pressing her palms into the damp dirt to elevate herself. Jackie called out.

"Hello!"

She was answered only with the lightness of silence, one reflecting not loneliness but rather peace. Jackie did not understand, if she had learnt that the one thing missing in her life was a deep connection with others, why should she learn how to be alone? Her question needed an answer. Jackie dipped into the lake, cool water darkening her hair and seeping into the pockets of her jeans. She swam to the tree in the middle, then stood beside it.

"All this, you get to see all day. The flowers smiling from the grass, the frogs swimming and the birds flying, the wind shaking the bushes."

The tree did not reply.

"All this, you get to hear all day. The songs, the flapping wings. The bubbling as water hits a rock and diverts its path."

The tree shook its branches, twigs jingling when they tapped one another. It noted that it was listening to her.

Jackie continued, "is my lesson, then, to stand alone and watch it all? Is that how to achieve peace? Never blooming, never growing myself, but existing humbly in a beautiful world? Tell me, for I have spent a lifetime blaming my unquenched misery when I should have instead been seeking guidance. Is this the final stop of the train?"

Jackie tried to turn her neck back from the scene and towards the tree but found that she could do no more than move her arms, now branches, to show that she listened. Beside her, a woman, hands wrapped around the strings of a backpack, walked to the tree's face and spoke in a voice Jackie recognised as her own.

"I have nothing to tell you that you do not know yourself already. I have long since stood here and had my eyes closed to the flowers and the birds. I did not notice their joys, did not know how to connect with them. You, who sought guidance on happiness, knew more of my own happinesses than me."

Jackie could not speak. She shook her branches again.

"Stay a while, won't you? Now I have one to stand tall with me and admire the view. The view that I could not see before you arrived."

In her mind, Jackie did not even consider the option. She shook her branches harder, and harder, more violently now, begging the tree to take back its form and let her reunite with herself, and her friends once more. The tree in Jackie's body looked to her sadly.

"Alright, I accept. You have others that need you. Come visit me again."

"How should I leave?"

Jackie's body stood amidst the oasis, able to move but not break out of the mirage. The tree ceased to speak, and stillness engulfed the scene. The river didn't flow, the bugs stopped chirping and singing. No birds flew above her head.

The wind returned for a moment, this time guiding the body with a soft push into the water. She felt herself fall, cold liquid covering her skin, yet instead of swimming she emerged on the other side completely whole. It was as if there had been no water, nothing touching her, but rather a falling of her soul back into her physical form. Her voice, her body, her mind, they were all entirely hers once more, flowing veins and every moving joint now a part that she was now grateful for. As Jackie opened her eyes, she stood in the city of Roskilde at night. The buildings, the illuminated cathedral, they were just as they had been. Yet now she saw them not as different, foreign and frightening, but rather welcoming. As if every path was constructed with people in mind, guiding them to where they needed to go. As if every building was built to be a home, every shop opened to bring a smile to a stranger.

There was a beauty in the unknown. Thus Jackie, having walked to the train station to find that the trains were running again, sat in her carriage marvelling at the countryside around her. She noticed how the vibrating hum of the train tickled her nose every time the train changed pace. Home, love, these were beyond concepts. She could feel now how she missed her family, her partner. Jackie travelled east towards Copenhagen, her speeding train chasing the rising sun, melting away into the colours and light which overwhelmed the sky.

Picking up the phone in a show of strength, Jackie watched her finger dial Ben's number. She didn't remember what time it was in New York. She didn't care. She wanted him to know she'd made a mistake and that she was finally ready to accept it. She wanted it not to be too late, and at the same time she knew that she would be ready to accept if it was. Jackie didn't want her anxiety to validate her anymore, to live with deafening thoughts of insecurity leading her every move. She wanted to be afraid, to put herself out there, and to feel the love even if for a brief moment.

"Jackie," came a familiar voice.

"Ben."

"I knew you'd call." She could hear his smile, the way his teeth sank into his lip when he was excited.

"I want to talk about us. I'm coming back home," she said confidently. "Let's meet. I miss you."

Fire

The year was 2087. On a late, autumn evening in central London, the sun set over the skyline as trees shed their leaves, waves of orange and brown washing over the city. As leaves got whisked up by the wind, they tasted freedom with a short journey through the hot sky. Eventually they were torn to insignificant pieces by the flying motor of a delivery drone, whirring in a rush to push freshly printed letters into office mailboxes. Ever since summer of the previous year, when the teenage generation created an internet movement to revive the printing press, doting parents and hungry businessmen alike pitched in to develop the drones. They were not yet perfected, but time is money, and so the drones flew choppily while swift hands signed an ever-increasing number of contracts with their partners. Even at night the mail drones were relentless. As the cold darkness approached, streets grew quiet for dinnertime, most of London already at home tucking their children in on a school night or resting with an overflowing glass of red wine to forget that they still had a lifetime of work remaining. If one was particularly observant, he would know that at eight thirty on weekday evenings, the ad-screens were turned off for the calm hour between families coming home and partygoers going out. For that hour, the sides of buildings no longer tracked for victims to scream AI-voiced advertisements to. It was a short break from the blazing cold, white light that followed people's eyelines for the remainder of the day. On every street corner, at every turn, they would usually be ready to sell a useless product to an unsuspecting passerby. Unless, of course, one was patient enough to hide in the office until eight thirty.

During this time the city softened into its old image of glory, before the fifth technology revolution of 2044. Back when printed newspapers were more than an internet trend, extracted from the minds of youth through eye-tracking technologies, but instead a way to stay informed about the world and all its possibilities. It is precisely in this quiet window that the journalist departed. As the day melted into night, he wandered the empty streets, letting the buzz of drones sound like the flapping wings of doves. He walked to the old-style bar, shielding his mind and seeking refuge from his distorted, plastic world.

The old-style bar was one of few spots remaining where the journalist could find true peace from his work. Technology was forbidden there, and so he did not have to wince at observing those around him scroll away from the news, knee-deep in advertisements indistinguishable from real content. That was to say that real content still existed, which was unlikely. Just this week, his thoroughly researched, fact-checked work had been shut down immediately, deemed uninteresting.

NEWS: The climate economy - a solution? Or just more water thrown onto a grease fire?

September 22nd, 2087. Independent News Company - Anonymous Journalist.

If you ask the question: What does our future look like? All popular media today will tell you that the future is safely secured, with expert scientists from all around the world having figured out the perfect solution to climate change: the climate economy. New technology has made it possible for us to retain previous levels of consumption, wealth, and economic growth while saving the world from the disastrous effects of climate change. Why then, have we seen rapidly rising temperatures around the equator, with warnings of deadly hurricanes and typhoons daily, and extreme freezes forcing previously-inhabited parts of Russia, Canada and Greenland to become entirely deserted? What of the rising tides and heat waves which have devastated Africa, South America, and coastal Asia? Today I sat down with the leading expert on economics and sustainability, the infamous Professor McRawls. Professor McRawls was recently fired from his position at a prominent University for his controversial work, after defying repeated government orders to shut down his research. What they couldn't shut down, however, was his desire to tell the truth.

Interviewer: It's an honour to have you here, sir.

McRawls: Thank you for having me.

Interviewer: I want to get started on the most important question, the one to make headlines for the rest of humanity's future. You have been researching climate policy effects for the past fifty years, comparing and predicting the past and future effects of each solution to climate change that the government has proposed. We are in a time of crisis, our world on the brink of apocalypse. The majority of Southeast Asia, South America, and Australia has sunk, killing billions of people and sending millions more into Europe as climate refugees. Governments all over the world committed to the 2079 London Pact claiming to save us all: the climate economy, which generates negative carbon emissions via consumer spending. It has been hailed by a plethora of sponsored experts. As a neutral observer, who only wants to tell the truth, I have only one question for you. The fate of the world rests on your honesty.

Professor, my question is this: how much time do we have left? Has the climate economy been effective, and will it still be effective?

McRawls: I am sorry to inform you of this. The climate economy has been a complete failure. While parts of Europe will remain inhabitable, we can expect that the next wave of extreme heat and ice will kill another billion people by stranding them in uninhabitable land. Europe, North America, and Central Asia, which will mostly survive this wave, are already overcrowded with refugees and will not be able to take in more without significantly compromising their living standards. People, crowded in bunkers with insufficient food and water, would now have to share even more of their few resources. It is inhumane, the treatment that they have been put through. We have all been lied to by leaders who wished to take no accountability and sought only to enrich themselves. Soon, it will be too late.

Interviewer: How long do we have until the next wave?

McRawls: My closest estimation is two weeks. I will break down the exact numbers and figures now, to help your

"Not enough clicks," the bot had beeped, before deleting his article.

Now only he knew what was coming for the climate market, and by consequence the world, but there was nothing he could do to stop it. The average person didn't understand the deals made behind closed doors, how the elites really functioned. There was no use announcing that anarchy would soon descend. They wouldn't understand until it was time to revolt, to join all those who were wronged by the elites in protest. That pivotal moment had not yet been reached. Now, those who could understand the incoming crisis would forget seconds later when they swiped away. Such was the curse of the new, fast media cycle, his truth lost amidst a thousand other truths, his words obsolete. He knew, however, that the moment would certainly come. He believed it for a single purpose; it kept him sane knowing that justice would be served.

As the journalist entered his favourite bar, the jazz music playing inside made him think of *her* again.

Often, she came here, though not often enough for them to meet. He had not seen his old partner in months, not since she betrayed their plan to conspire against their firm and stole his research. He recalled that day now, walking into the bar slowly, hopefully, closing the door on the outside world. In the street behind him an unbearable grinding was heard, metal brakes squealing frightfully as the new metro halted. He'd written an article some weeks ago regarding its cheap construction, that in an attempt to cut costs, substandard materials had been used. In detail, he proved how an insufficient number of unskilled workers fought to meet an impossible deadline, even going out of his way to locate those who were unafraid to testify. The entire process took over a month, not only fact-checking his piece but also ensuring that the identities of all civilians involved were protected. In the end, the metro had been built, and the journalist's article was the only thing it had killed so far. Regardless, he always walked. Far too dangerous to use the metro. It could blow at any time. As he shut the door to the bar and heard the cart's heavy push of acceleration, he left his stress behind.

The jazz ensemble played, music loud now that he was close to the band. Orange light illuminated the warm room, showcasing a variety of art. Portraits, landscapes, and sculptures protruded from the walls, a mixture of semi-human faces and natural scenes, a pleasing blend of abstract ideas in a classical style. New ideas conformed to the known practices of the old days, letting them improve and supplement but not overtake. As the journalist traced the walls with his eyes, his gaze settled on a different form of art, a customer inside the bar.

A woman in a silk dress danced, dazzling, burgundy fabric stretched over her breasts and waist tightly like the tension of a water's surface, staying close to her as she moved. Her feet tapped against the floor. Her arms reached above her head and painted, red fingernails traced the bare skin of her neck, then following her silhouette. Down the shoulders, across each arm walked the fingers. Down her waist. The journalist wanted to be embarrassed, to stop staring, but he was entirely mesmerised. There was a perfect synergy between her and the tune.

What was lacking, however, was synergy between the woman and the furniture. When she took a sudden step, the table beside her rumbled, shaking an old, gin bottle used to hold a dripping candlestick. Instinctively, the journalist stepped forward to catch the candle if it fell, but as he did so he bumped his head into an antique lamp which hung from the ceiling. It wobbled from side-to-side as he awkwardly stabilised it, resting his hands on the flower patterns of the tinted glass. The woman looked up; luscious, red lips parted softly in mild surprise. She recognised him immediately. Stunned, the journalist hurried away, ordering a drink from the bar on his way.

The bartender poured whiskey into a chilled, crystal glass. Through its diamond-patterns, he noticed the reflection of the approaching red figure. The warning was feeble, however, as by the time he acknowledged that she was coming, he already felt her body beside him. Unable to escape, he shifted in his seat, and they came face-to-face, his lips mere centimetres away from the tip of her nose. As he twisted to move his body away, a button popped open from his crisp, white shirt, revealing his skin, vibrantly dark and smooth like velvet.

"Well, that's a warm welcome," she laughed quietly, gentle and careful, aware of their closeness.

Her eyes lingered on the hair bursting through the naked gap between the white fabric, ignoring his hands which rushed to pull the shirt back together.

"Now, now. Don't do that. Come and dance with me instead," she purred, a thin strap of her red dress slipping off her shoulder.

He scoffed in response, confidence regained from the energy that his annoyance brought. The liquid in his glass seeped into his mouth, bitter and cold. He was afraid of her smell, to remember the warmth of her skin and the feel of her hair against his neck. More than he feared the doomed world, he was terrified of letting her have a hold over him again.

A wild glimmer could be seen in her eye as she pouted mockingly. He wondered if the persona was real. Her words were sharp, but he had seen many facades in the past. Was she so different now, had greed overcome her entirely, or was there still something remaining of the kind, gentle woman he'd known and loved?

"You know I had to kill the article. You would have done the same if you were a better businessman. A loss of faith in the government would be far too dangerous.

The climate economy is fragile, and it relies on investment from the public."

"You mean, it relies on sapping money from the public," he turned away.

"Losing it could destabilise us all." She spun his chair back, unable to leave him in peace. The rosemary scent in her hair overpowered the whiskey's bitterness. She looked so innocent, eyes glancing up at him like she used to do before a long, sweet kiss. Bitter from the long nights of working for a victory that ended up stolen, he leaned further from her charm. The algorithms had been controlled. She hadn't denied it. There were still so many more questions, so much more to say. He wanted never to see her again, and simultaneously couldn't bear to look away.

"Tell me one thing."

"Sure." She grabbed the glass and took a sip before continuing, leaving a lipstick stain on the rim and filling the silent moment with tension. "Anything for you."

Before asking, their past and their stolen future flashed through his mind. Here she stood, just as she did when they'd catch up for a drink in the old bar, the happy memory imbued forever in the vintage chandelier. He remembered how they had worked together, vowing to take control of the market and turn it into a force for good. She, the energy chemist, had been the first to understand the real impact of the shady deals. He, the economist, fit both personal financial effects and the macroeconomic outcomes neatly together. It was a perfectly fitting puzzle. No doubt about it, she discovered that the removal of carbon from the atmosphere through the carbon economy project did not work. Beyond that, he saw that elites were dependent on the project failing, on the numbers not adding up, in order to pocket maximum profit due to low operating costs of the failed programme. The International Gas and Oil Authority was both the place they'd met as coworkers from distant teams, and the place they put their minds together and understood how to transform the global future. The formulas she'd developed, and the strategies he was ready to negotiate, it was all ready. Standing here, in the old bar, the image of her in the past, sweetly smiling under her lab coat, melted away. What was left was the thief who had doomed the planet. He was not afraid to ask.

"I know why you sided with the money. Why lead me on for so long though? Why build up the project in the first place? Why…" As his voice grew faint, she interrupted the final question, the most important one.

"You think I sided with the money? Is that it?" Her voice was shrill and angry, a small scream.

The music stopped abruptly. They realised now that they were the last two people in the bar, except for the band and the bartender. No one dared interrupt the conversation.

"Of course you sided with the money!"

"And if I'd stayed with you, then what? You'd give me equal credit, we'd get married, live happily ever after? No, no, no! Either you know that's not what would happen and you're purposefully winding me up, or you actually think that's what you would do, but it's not! I was a nobody! A puny, little, young chemist who had just come off studying into a company placement. You were an established authority. You had so many papers published, everyone knew your name. I would have given up everything, everything for you and it never would've been equal."

"For me? For the world! The world that you doomed!"

"I didn't doom anyone or anything! Why is it up to me to save everyone? I had a job, I had a good life. You were going to take it all away!"

"I was trying to save us," he spat, anger bubbling in his throat.

"You were trying to save yourself! You were using me to do it."

"You traded me in for a bunch of crooks."

"Yes! Yes I did!" She laughed deliriously. "Better the devil you know, than the devil you don't! That's how the saying goes, isn't it? The power you had over me, it was intoxicating. One day I woke up with a hangover from you, and I knew I was wasting my life for your dream of saving the world."

"Would you choose yourself over the entire world?"

"I already did." Tears streamed down her face. Her anger had exploded into deep, deep sadness.

"What happened to us?" His words were slow, each heavy syllable pouring from his tongue like bitter whiskey. "Why didn't you love me?"

"I loved you with everything I had. You, you loved the world over me. Over all of us. We could have had such good lives together, and you gave it all up for a self-sacrificing project. It wouldn't have worked."

"It could have!"

"It wouldn't have! Not in the world we live in. Someone would have paid someone off. Besides, I did us all a favour anyway. Look at you, fancy journalist now."

"You think that the answer to a broken future is to break the present too?"

"It's not that simple!" she exclaimed in frustration.

Yet she didn't continue to explain. Her mouth gaped open, lacking words. Mascara smudged down her face from tears, hair tangled from the tossing of her aching, anxious neck, she headed back towards the band. Upon her command, they resumed playing the song. The smooth tune took the journalist by the heart, and he found himself led to follow her. He hated her. He was trying to hate her. He still loved her. He didn't want her to go, because he loved her. The answer was there, all along. The words she'd asked him to say, before she had leaked the news and got him fired. The words he hadn't said, that ruined everything.

The floor faded away around her, music dissipating as her heels tapped against the dark wood. She was all he saw and heard, consuming him, pulling his gut through his mouth like she had done over, and over again in the years he'd known her. He'd believed back then that it was his fault, and he was choking with the force of wanting to believe her now. No longer able to fight the desire for his body to move with the music, to follow her in dancing to the song. It was a tune he had etched on his heart, sewed through his body and to his fingertips, his skin longing for hers.

Blindly, arms outstretched, he walked towards her. His fingers wrapped around her waist, pulling her into him, kissing a single sentence into her ear.

"I love you."

She began to cry again. The music played, and they danced in unison, the way two people can only do when their bodies are embedded with the weight of a joint mistake.

"I have always loved you," he whispered.

"I'm sorry. It was all me, my insecurity, my fear. I-."

"Shhhhh, you don't need to tell me. I know," he shushed her, and they continued to dance.

Outside, the citizenry screamed and rioted. Somehow, the journalist's article had made headlines. They found out about the climate economy, about the doom. The damage was officially irreversible, and their lives would never be free of the fire again. All their work, all their investment and all their livelihood had been for nothing, as all the meanwhile tyrants were ensuring that they poisoned more of the planet than collective action could save. Their current system would be overthrown before long, and the chemist with it.

The chemist smiled at the journalist, shocking him.

"Seems my friend in the media team finally got a certain email," she laughed.

So they had not met in the bar by accident. He grinned and grabbed her tightly, holding her even closer than before. The disguise was up, for both of them. Her cold, silky skin coated his, her presence made him burn up a fever. Her eyes were a deep green, a void revealing her past self and her vibrant, fresh hopes. Perhaps her silent gaze, her longing dance, was her way of telling him that nothing had changed. That she, too late, had accounted now for her mistake. He spun her, stopping a hundred and eighty degrees into the turn and fitting his head into the crane of her neck. She gasped, off-guard.

"I know that you tried your best. We all did," he murmured, hugging her closely.

She did not break apart from him until he spun her again, kissing her, huge tears covering both their faces. Outside, the drones shrieked *FIRE*. Electric cars were set ablaze. People scaled buildings and threw bricks through company headquarter windows. The train tracks stopped squealing as the wheels that previously scratched against them, were ripped off the train's body. Violent passion erupted. Screens smashed, lights dying out. Inside the bar, the journalist wrapped himself around the chemist knowingly. Her skin against his burning hands, their worlds were already on fire.

Bones of the Survivors

A remote village in the Russian Empire's countryside. Pre-WWI.

Ekaterina (Katya) Milova, seven years old, stood in front of a swing in the single, tiny, playground built in the city. Abandoned benches lined the square, where parents never sat to watch their children. It was not a time of leisure, of enjoyment. Routine was necessary and laughter was taboo. There were four pieces of heavy, metal equipment painted in various colours; a slide approximately four metres in height, a swing, a see-saw, and a rocking horse whose spring creaked in pain whenever children rode it. Ekaterina's favourite was the slide, but it was currently occupied by two boys for whom her dislike outweighed her love for the slide. She considered arguing with them for access to the slide. She was fatigued, worn out from the action of the morning, and wanted the comfort of her favourite activity before it grew late. If she waited much longer, the sun would set. Ekaterina did not want to slide into the darkness.

She pulled her jacket down over her bottom as her mother frequently instructed, and felt herself sink into the swing's chipped, wooden seat. Her frail fingers wrapped halfway around the thick, metal bar and she began swaying, using the unidentifiable muscles in her back to push backwards and forwards until sufficient momentum was gathered and the swing sailed through the air. Backwards and forwards. Backwards and forwards. Ekaterina rocked on the swing like a pendulum, watching as birds weaved through the grey sky, feathered bodies effortlessly hooking themselves onto the wind. She pushed harder, swinging further and faster, the wind catching onto her braided hair and slicing through her jacket. She was not afraid when the fabric ripped and her sleeves were pulled back into the air, catching the wind perfectly like wings. She let the harsh gusts scratch her face as they lifted her in the air, her jacket expanding, rising upwards like a balloon. Ekaterina watched herself in the air, amazed, adrenaline rushing through her body in a heat that made her forget the violent wind. It whisked her up suddenly, and she was catapulted towards the birds. This was what she had wanted. She thought of her father's service, his flowing cloak as he walked up the steps to share the words of God. Flowing white, just like the clouds. Was it part of her duty to explore the skies?

"Take me with you," she begged the birds as her tiny body continued to glide upwards. This was her meaning. Ekaterina rose higher, and higher, a light enveloping her as her hand reached for the birds. Clouds washed away as she hurled faster through the sky. Too fast. She missed the birds and spun into the horizon. She was a whirlwind now, watching herself spin and shake to create bullets of wind that hurled towards the city, pulsing through the air and knocking down buildings as they hit. It was happening again. Bombs hit the city and bullets embedded themselves in the soft bodies of people, and Ekaterina could do nothing but scream as she fell from the sky. She closed her eyes and began to whisper a prayer, just as she had been taught.

"Katya, are you alright?" Mikhail (Misha) Shuysky, a nine-year-old boy who lived next-door, stood leaning over her as she opened her eyes. Ekaterina lay on her back, embedded in the dirt. She had survived the fall.

"What happened?" she asked, still dizzy.

"You shouldn't jump out of the swing, Katya. You could hurt yourself like that."

"I didn't jump. God took me away to teach me a lesson."

"Don't lie, Katya. Your father will punish you," Mikhail said with concern.

"I'm not lying, Misha. Something is coming."

"You spend too much time thinking. You should go home and wash your coat. It's a better use of your time."

"Okay," she said before running down the dirt path, sleet squelching under her boots. Water entered through a small rip she'd never told her mother about. Had it been shame, the fear of taking up space in her mother's world, already so frail?

At home, she sat alone and ate a single portion of bread. An oak table and three chairs of the same wood, one designated for each member of the remains of their small family, accompanied her. Dinner was not a meal allocated to everyone equally, not on days like this. Her mother returned from visiting the neighbour, loosening Ekaterina's hair from the braid it had been in and running the strands between her icy fingers. Brushing through the tangles gently, she braided the smooth again. The hairstyle was tight despite the mother's trembling hands, and she left in silence when the braid was complete while her child picked crumbs of bread from the table and licked them off her fingers diligently.

*

"So, what's coming?" Mikhail sat on one end of a see-saw, looking up, and then down, at Ekaterina.

"What?"

"Nothing." The see-saw creaked as it balanced them on each end before briefly sinking him to the ground.

"Misha, what are you talking about?"

"Yesterday you said there was something coming. I want to know what it is." Mikhail swung up again.

"I thought you didn't believe me."

"I don't. I think you're just a dumb girl."

"Why do you want to know, then?" She stopped the see-saw with one foot, leaving Mikhail hanging in the air. Ekaterina hadn't previously thought herself capable of lifting a boy like this.

"To be prepared. Just in case. It's always better to know than not to know, isn't it? What if I need to take care of my mother while my father is out working? What if we're sitting here and an alien comes out of the sky and I need to push you out of the way, you know?" Misha realised suddenly that he was suspended in the air, and quickly grumbled at Ekaterina to let him down.

"It's not aliens, Misha." They sat now, balancing with their feet on the ground in unison.

"Well, that's why I'm asking. It's your own fault for not telling me what it is."

"That's because I don't know."

"Then why are you babbling on about it?"

"I'm not, you were the one that asked me."

"No, I didn't!"

"Yes, you did!"

"Well how do you even know that something is coming if you don't know what it is?"

"Aren't you hungry, Misha?" She posed the question so innocently, with an honest heart that only a child could have. Tears pooled in Mikhail's eyes. Despair painfully filled the gap reserved for anger, a blind rage which could numb him. Numb him like it numbed the hunger. Mikhail had used up all his anger, it seemed. Sharply darting his head away from her, he stumbled off his seat and ran away, kicking up sand in his path.

"No! No, I'm not! I'm not hungry! God will make sure I am not hungry, as he does for you!"

The unbalanced seesaw dropped Ekaterina and sand seeped in through the seam of her boot. She watched Mikhail run, his arms desperately swinging at each side and his knees bending to support the weight of his body. He moved more clumsily than he had before, his knee locking into itself as he fell to the ground in injury. He lay there for many seconds before pushing himself up with a single, trembling arm, using the sleeve of the other to wipe away tears and snot. Mikhail looked back a single time, and despite the distance between them, his expression was unmistakably pained. He rose and limped around the corner, his body disappearing behind houses of thick, heavy planks of wood and tiny windows. Ekaterina sat alone with damp sand in her boot and a single question echoing within her.

*

Yaroslav Milov was sat at the table when Ekaterina showed up home later, her face covered in soot. His giant beard and moustache shook as he talked, coming close to her only to tie a *platok* scarf around her head, the fabric tight against her scalp and neck. Ekaterina had only a few other notable belongings.

"But Papa, why?" she begged, starting to sob. "Where is Mama?"

"She will join you soon." Yaroslav looked down on his daughter. "Chin up, Ekaterina. You are not a baby to be crying like this. Do not humiliate me. You will refer to her as Zabava Yevgenyevna, with her patronymic name, as it is proper."

Yaroslav walked out the door without taking her hand and watched from the entrance of their house as his only living daughter met Zabava Dayneko and walked out of his life. After a few moments, he set off for the church. Whether or not his daughter looked back tearfully as she went, whether or not he heard her calls and cries, she was not his concern for the time being. He had a duty to fulfil. How long it took Ekaterina and Zabava to wade off-path into the forest, to disappear behind towering pines whose needles reached out to pinch the child, he did not know. Instead, Yaroslav looked to the church, the most fortified building in the town, its strong body of red brick, bauble hands that curved and reached towards the sky, and stained, glass window-eyes with arching lids that watched him incessantly.

*

Zabava was a tall woman in her late twenties, her face a map of tiny wrinkles, considered old and plump for the standards of the area. Zabava walked more quickly than the child could handle, big feet in torn-up boots that took huge steps and would not wait for Ekaterina if she fell behind. She had a round face and large breasts that filled Ekaterina with embarrassed curiosity. She had not seen a person who ate enough to have such breasts in her entire seven years of life, and it made her daydream about a land of feasts with meat and birds like tales her mother used to tell. Before Yaroslav had forbidden the stories.

Ekaterina had stopped wailing an hour into their walk through the forest, and Zabava finally decided that the child had earned the right to be acknowledged.

"Don't stare at me. What is the matter with you?" Her voice was deep and cracked frequently, and a piece of hair fell out of her *platok* as she turned to face Ekaterina.

"Zabava Yevgenyevna, can I ask you a question?" she sniffled.

"Fine."

"Where are we going?"

"Don't ask me a question that you already know the answer to. People don't like to have their time wasted."

Ekaterina took a moment to think, and asked, "will there be other children?"

"Five."

"Will Misha be there?"

"No."

"Why?"

"That's more than one question," she sighed. "Five children. Sascha, Yuri, Mila, Elisey, Lev."

"Zabava Yevgenyevna, why won't..." Ekaterina began but was interrupted.

"Katya, no need for the formalities. You can call me *Tetya* Zabava."

"Are you my real *tetya*?"

Zabava stopped and lifted Ekaterina off the ground swiftly, the extent of her strength evident to the child immediately. She must have been the largest, strongest woman Ekaterina had ever encountered.

"If I had a chair here, or a place to sit, I would bend you over my knee and beat you for that question."

Ekaterina looked at her sadly.

Zabava walked onwards, muttering the answer to Ekaterina's question to herself, "of course not. Barely any of us have enough family left for that."

Just as the dark began to twist its fingers through the trees to overshadow rays of fading sun, they reached Zabava's house. It was one storey in height, made of round, walnut-shaded columns stacked horizontally over each other to form a rectangular base with softened corners. The roof was covered in snow, and the tiny carved-out windows were impossible to see into for the lack of light, both outside and inside the house. Ekaterina entered silently, the giant Zabava looming behind her like a prison warden. An uncarpeted hallway scattered with various winter gear led into a large room, a dining area where people sat and an open kitchen with a large stove. Depictions of holy figures lined a single wall in the room. Six faces, brightened by candlelight, looked up from their meal in unison. Five children and another woman, with thick hair and no *platok*, left free to roam the room as it pleased. It reached for the ceiling and did not budge an inch when the woman rose to greet Ekaterina. She was almost as tall as Zabava.

"My younger sister," Zabava explained, "Marina Dayneko."

"Good evening. Would you like some food?" Marina picked up a pair of child's boots from the floor and tucked them away into a shelf. She motioned for Ekaterina to put her own shoes there, and the girl obliged silently.

Upon not receiving a response, Marina went into the kitchen and procured a plate, filled with a soup of potatoes, carrots and beets, along with a piece of bread on the side.

"Come, eat."

"Thank you." Ekaterina sat beside a girl a year or two older than her and began to eat nervously. She couldn't help but admire that the soup was more fulfilling than anything she had eaten in weeks, and later scolded herself for thinking this.

As time passed and Ekaterina settled into her new life, the days began to feel shorter, passing by a little faster with each rising sun. She shared a room with the other two girls, while the boys had another that she was forbidden to venture into. During the day they alternated in working on Zabava's tiny farm, in a greenhouse two metres in length that she and Marina had built themselves from scraps of an abandoned building project nearby. When it was left behind, so were they. Unmonitored and remote, they managed to avoid their greenhouse being confiscated by bureaucrats or terrorised by gangs. They went unnoticed and were able to avoid the work that the rest of the townsfolk did, managing to keep the fruits of their labour without having them stolen. Zabava and her sister's two children took on a few orphans under care of the church, increasing the size of their shaky and uncertain family. Now, Ekaterina was here. Another worker and another mouth to feed. They grew a few root vegetables and traded them for bread, as well as keeping some for themselves. There were no feasts, barely enough to support themselves. Staying alive was the only thing they could think of. Working hard one day only left them knowing that they had the privilege of waking up another day and working harder.

Yet alongside the fear and endless work, there were miniscule moments of joy. Laughter echoed through the house as Ekaterina told stories to the other girls of her life in the centre of town, of her mother's fairytales and her days with Mikhail at the playground. They imagined days before the hunger began, and the stories brought hope that it would end someday too. She began to dream again, without fear of sleeping. Blocked in a bubble away from the fearful world, Ekaterina stopped wanting to ask questions. She prayed for better days, but the burden of her pain lightened.

*

On the Sunday two weeks after Ekaterina's relocation, Zabava brought all the children to church service. Yaroslav led, as was custom, and Ekaterina watched him for the first time not as her father but only as her priest. There was a new distance between them, beyond physical. It was as if she had lived a parallel life in his absence. He did not look thinner, but many others did. Mikhail was not present, but his parents were. They looked ill and sallow.

"What are you doing?" Ekaterina had snuck out and now stood by a crate tucked behind a curtain close to the church entryway. It was hidden, but not entirely unnoticeable, and a woman with her dark hair in long, thin braids was crouched over, placing potatoes inside the crate.

"Go away, kid," she murmured before recognizing the voice of who she was speaking to. "Oh, Ekaterina. Be

99

a good girl and let your father know we've got donations for him."

"Why are you giving away your food? Are you not hungry?" Ekaterina asked curiously.

The woman rose slowly, struggling to balance and straightening up only when her hand pressed against the wall. Her fingers were bony and battered, her blue-toned skin was dry and flaky, covered in inflamed, rough patches. There were multiple gaps in her teeth and red, puffy eyelids devoured her eyes.

"I won't be hungry for long, little girl." She blinked excessively while scratching a rash on her cheek with a skinny finger that was missing a nail. It began to bleed.

"Your face, it's... there's blood..." Ekaterina gasped.

The woman cackled, "well that's a good sign. It means I am still alive, after all. I wasn't sure."

Removing her blistered palm from the wall, the woman took clumsy, swaying steps back inside the large hall. The potatoes stared at the child menacingly from inside the crate, and Ekaterina quickly pulled the curtain forward to hide them before running outside. She looked at the high windows of the church.

"Was she a witch?" Ekaterina whispered with horror, her eyes darting in all directions. *"Baba Yaga."*

Outside she stood, mulling over her own discomfort for just under an hour. The trees around the church were stripped of their bark and the small amount of surviving grass was matted and ripped. Who had done this? Why? Marina, Zabava and the other children walked out and Zabava began to yell at her for leaving the service early. Zabava brought out a sack from her coat, going back inside the church, before returning outside with its contents shaking and bumping against each other.

"What's inside the bag, *tetya*?"

"I've had just about enough of you. Let's go, Ekaterina," Zabava snapped.

"Why are we stealing from other people?" Tears welled in her eyes, and they would not stop, her voice growing louder. "I thought we grew our own food, I don't understand."

"Ekaterina enough."

"I don't understand. Why?"

Zabava snatched the child and slung her over her shoulder, hissing, "you're causing a scene. Don't accuse me of evil for keeping you alive."

"Why me?" Ekaterina whimpered, and it was the only sentence she could say, over and over again, until she struggled her way out of Zabava's arms and fell to the ground. Her tiny body was bashed against the dirt, but the girl was strong despite her little frame, and so she got up and ran out of Zabava's grasp.

"Should I-" Marina began.

"No," Zabava replied firmly, "let her be. Being ungrateful is her own choice and she will suffer for it."

When she separated from the group at the church, Ekaterina had only one place in her mind that could bring her comfort.

Ekaterina sat on the swing once more, having run away at the church left her with no home to go to. She could not return to her father, nor was she ready to face the punishment of returning to Zabava. She didn't want the other children to see her differently, and so she hid in an unchanged part of town, pretending that her life was the same as the day she fell off the swing. She longed to hear her mother running after her playfully, to see her smile. Ekaterina wished to feel a human touch not born of a survivor's desperate violence.

A boy of a similar age approached her. His balding head bobbled as he walked unevenly, gasping for air as if exhausted despite the slow pace. The boy's stomach was bloated, and his coat could not zip properly.

"Misha? Is that really you?" She prayed he would say no.

"Katya. It's been so long. Though I knew you would be alright." His breath smelled of rot.

"What happened, Misha? What's wrong with our town? People are disappearing and those that remain are so sick, sick like you are."

"You already know, Katya," he breathed. "I lied before, when I said I wasn't hungry. I hope God can forgive me for my lies. I hope you, too, can forgive me."

"Misha, you have to come with me." Ekaterina hopped from the swing, landing firmly in her boots. She pulled at his hand and the boy crumpled, his knees sinking into the sand. She sat to meet him at eye level.

"Misha, we must go. I live in a house with a *tetya* who can help you. Come with me."

"No, Katya," he cried. "Don't you understand? Our donations, they were for you and for the priest's family. They will protect you through hunger. It is the will of God."

Katya recoiled, standing up. She offered the boy a hand and he raised his frail body so slowly that he could have been made of gold.

"Why, Misha? We are both just people."

"No, Katya. It is my duty to protect you." He winced from the pain of smiling. "Goodbye, Ekaterina Milova."

Ekaterina did not return to Zabava until the next morning, with a dirty, red face and eyes swollen from tears. Even then there were no words sufficient to close the rift torn between them.

*

Winter passed. Years went on. Many that were there before, were there no longer. It was beyond a ghost town, hollow to the core, even memories seemed to be wiped. Ghosts struggle to exist when their stories are untold. Zabava's children survived, malnourished and fighting through every day. Ekaterina knew that the first winter, they had not grown enough to truly feed themselves. Space in their haven was limited. This was how they survived.

The town slowly revived. Trade came with their neighbours in larger towns, and movement grew steady between those towns and growing cities. Life settled. Children were born. The church was destroyed under the new regime, and on nights when no one was around, Ekaterina woke up to weep. It was as if her very limbs had been severed, her tether to the past demolished and scrapped for materials. She never moved back to her father's home, though she passed by often and silently wished for him to walk out and see that his daughter still lived. Once, he did, standing at the door and staring at her ghost, his face hidden behind untidy, grown-out hair. His eyes were deep with heartbreak. She could do nothing but turn and walk away, just as his lips parted with hope for the right words to come.

Ekaterina resided with Zabava and Marina in their found family until she was the first of the children to turn 16, leaving for education in Moscow. On her 19th birthday, she visited her hometown for the first time since leaving. Her maturity had outgrown the fear. Zabava led her into the town square, where a concrete tablet stood in place of the church, over two metres in height. Names had been etched into it, and varieties of flowers and other offerings lay underneath. A knitted scarf was torn and murky from the brown sleet on the path. Ekaterina read her mother's name on the tablet, and Mikhail's. Many others she also recognized. A hand flew past her face and touched the tablet, tracing a dusty finger over the pristine grey.

"We could not save them." Yaroslav's clear voice boomed from behind her. It was the only reminiscence to the past that he got to keep.

"They are with the heavens now," Zabava responded. "Flying free like birds."

Neither Yaroslav nor Ekaterina wished to disagree. They stood for a long time, each aware that they alone had the ability to tether the past to the future. No newspaper would print their story, no history book would detail their lives, but at least for as long as each of them lived the past would not be forgotten.

Through the eyes of the Sun

I powdered the tip of young Mathilde's nose, handling her gently like a dove with a broken neck. She sat perfectly still, unsmiling, and I felt her porcelain face stiffen. Nothing had changed about my movements, but the footsteps of Henriette, her aunt, could be heard in the great hall two rooms over. This evidently bothered Mathilde. The hall was overly grand, a snobbish display of wealth. The chandeliers were far too large for the ceiling, hanging low like overripe fruits in the spring. Each painting's frame was grandiose, so extremely rich in detail and glimmering gold that it diluted the experience of looking at the art itself. Instead, looking at art became all about what possessing the art represented, money and privilege. The walls were dark with old paint, and the enormous rooms throughout the building loomed like voids, snatching a breath right from the lungs of each entering person. Young Mathilde's bedroom was smaller than most rooms here, yet its design did not differ from the rest of the residence, red-wine walls and an elevated, gold bed covered in layers upon layers of unused duvets. I partook in the huge effort to remove them each night, and along with two other maids I tucked them under the corners of the girl's mattress every morning, knowing that the work would be repeated pointlessly as long as she lived. Yet another reminder that none of my actions here mattered. I was entirely powerless. In the bedroom with Mathilde, the maids gradually sank into a place far from reality, far from the normality that sunlight could bring. Here the truth melted into the dark walls, hidden behind decor.

As I brushed Mathilde's makeup on, she regarded not herself in the mirror, but rather the curve of the doorway, waiting for her aunt to be within earshot. She was brewing up another one of her evil tricks.

"Stop this! You're hurting me, you rat!" She began to whine, flinching unconvincingly. I wasn't sure if Mathilde had ever been truly inconvenienced, let alone brought to the point of pain. It was thus only natural that she wouldn't know how to feign it.

"I apologise, Miss Mathilde," I recited calmly. This was the only way to speak to Mathilde, cruel snakes seeping through the cracks in her painted face, her words biting you at the first sign of defiance. She fed on this energy, on any expression of my discontent. Henriette's metal shoes grew louder, heavy steps approaching like the banging drums of the Royal Guards.

"What is this nonsense?" Henriette boomed, finally in the room.

"This maid is harming me! She's…" Mathilde was fighting to suppress her smirk.

"Mathilde, be silent." Henriette made firm eye contact with her niece. Her gaze cut a sharp line between me and them, and I exhaled knowing that I was symbolically far, far away. Henriette never paid any attention to me. Mathilde ceased speaking immediately, and tears welled in her eyes. I had to admit that this was a rather unusual scene, her aunt typically let her poke and prod me a little, even though I knew from overhearing late-night conversations that their pool of money was shrinking, and they could not afford to fire me and hire a more experienced replacement. Perhaps this was why her attitude changed on this day. Circumstance had played its cards and beat Mathilde out.

"Mathilde," Henriette said as she turned to leave the room, "you will behave well."

"But… I was only trying to…" Mathilde's whimper made the aunt turn her neck and ice us with her stare once more.

"Did I ask you a question?"

"No, Henriette."

"Good." She left, and I was alone with the girl once more. I felt a small victory, a triumph over this horrible, spoiled teenager who I'd had to be a personal maid to for the past four years. It was true, I was provided fair lodging and meals, as well as a small wage. I knew that only a few years remained before I could leave this mansion, take my savings with me and finally get married, having my own children who I would raise with more character and generosity than this entire family had ever shown themselves to be in possession of. I dreamt often of leaving, letting the idea soothe me while Mathilde would scream and pull my hair, and when she would complain about me to her aunt and leave me without my dinner as punishment.

"Ariel." Mathilde had been embarrassed for once. I wondered what she would do now.

"Yes, Miss Mathilde?"

"Stand up."

"Yes, Miss Mathilde." I stood obediently, waiting for her to slap me. She did no such thing.

"Come," she smiled, almost sweetly. Together we left her bedroom and turned to walk down a stairwell connecting the main areas of the house. The stairs were covered in a burgundy carpet, smooth velvet folding over like a wave of red blood. The walls, large due to the high ceilings, contained paintings of Mathilde's family stretching over generations, golden frames entwined with natural patterns. Unlike the collector's editions of famous European art in the rest of the house, the stairwell was dedicated to celebrating the family's dominance. Lions, gazelles and grand trees were embedded in the frames, each one custom-made and unique. Mathilde stopped me before a small likeness of her and her mother. Falling leaves surrounded the art, depicting a beautiful woman and a little girl beside her, rescuing a man that had fallen into a deep, green river. The woman's pale skin shone like the skin of an angel, and she appeared to be pulling the man into her light, out of the dark water.

Mathilde giggled, "she drowned him."

I gasped.

"Yes," she continued to laugh, her cackle growing wilder and more uncontrollable. "I watched her do it. An old servant, stupid fool, who had upset me. Mother wanted him punished."

"Oh." I couldn't breathe, my heart twisting and aching in my chest. My body felt the heaviness of grief, and an anger of the twisting of this story, of this heroic depiction of a horrible woman that would outlive anyone who knew the truth.

"So, we drowned him." Mathilde's cackle subsided, her eyes glistening with delight. "One day, I will do the same to you."

That night I did not sleep. For many nights, I could not, in part from the anger of being threatened by this puny, insufferable child who would never know a life without endless privilege. Days later, I rested in my bedchamber when I went to see Grandmother, an old performer for the family who retired years ago from old age and injury. While we were unrelated, and even though I knew very little about her at all, we were a kind of family here. Why she remained living in the servants' chambers, I did not dare to ask.

"What's wrong, my child?" Grandmother sat on the ground with a blanket spread over her lap, head tilted back, and eyes closed. The room was warmed by a single, thin candle standing on the tabouret beside her. She possessed the unique skill of reading people and could clearly feel my frustration without taking a single look.

"Why does she act like that?" I spat out a tangle of words, anger flowing through the veins in my face.

"Well, she has been given the opportunity."

"What does that mean?"

"Ariel, it is a blessing to me that you do not yet understand." Grandmother opened her eyes and sat up with impeccable posture, motioning for me to sit down beside her. Her atrophied muscles had the ghostly air of an old ballet dancer, the memory of being strong and graceful, in control of her own body completely. Before, she could leap, floating across the stage, bend herself into a variety of shapes with only a thought. She had been trained to make everything look easy, to hide the abuse and defer feeling the pain until the next day. I lowered myself onto the cold floor beside her worn body, and she continued to speak.

"There are some people in this world who are secret actors, conditioned from their childhood - perhaps a lack of love or the other, I am not to know - to sit and wait for the role of a lifetime. What role? Well, the role of the victim of course. The one who was wronged, the one most deserving of an extra blessing to make up for their misfortune. Now she becomes everything and you, to her, become nothing. Some kind of stone in the shoe that the world must kiss so that she may be whole again. People like that, my dear, they will unknowingly spend their lifetimes waiting, begging, praying." She paused for a short moment, one that the average person could have missed, her eyes darting upwards as the air containing the word 'praying' escapes her lips. I was always certain that she was raised religious.

Once, years ago, I'd asked why she never spoke about beliefs, why she never prayed.

"Because, dear, I am damned. The damned do not pray unless out of disrespect." Her feigned smile and glass eyes, too weak to hide years of pain, were enough to never make me ask again. Her very prayers, her own words had been ripped from her. Her thoughts were not her own, instead they were monitored to make sure she stood in line, was subservient. A

woman who could once perform, reduced to a statue, rotting her life away in a decorated cell.

Now, we sat in silence for a second before she realised her focus shifted.

"Do you understand? She has been waiting and will not let this go. You'd best ignore it for some time, now you are the short end to a funnel of hatred." She spoke solemnly, while simultaneously appearing not to take the issue all too seriously. As if this would be brushed off the next day.

"I am not strong like you," I replied quietly, my anger subsiding.

"No, I hope you will not have to be. Though you should know that a hard past does not make you strong but merely grinds at you, wearing you down. The abrasive surface comes from having the smooth and kindness moulded out of people like me. There is strength, too, in innocence." She smiled.

"Now, let's be off to bed soon. Your old grandmother has had a long day." I knew better than to inquire further. I let her leave secrets in the space between her and the sky, autonomy as the sole freedom that I may grant her.

That night, I dreamt of a woman from far away, summoned for Mathilde's family as a ballet performer. At the mere age of fourteen, she was bought from her family whom she would struggle to remember as she grew old and frail. She would spend her life at the beck and call of Mathilde's mother, still alive then, and her young sister Henriette. They loved to torment the dancer, forcing her to repeat jumps again and again until her feet bled through her shoes. Twisted ankles would be popped back into place and she would jump like a horse, a grand being whipped into shape. She would be awoken at odd times of the night, never allowed a peaceful respite so that her brain could not develop properly. They told her that she was a creature beneath them, poor without a family, and that she should have the physique to fit such an inhuman thing, branding her back and hips with the furnace iron. She belonged to them, and she would for life.

I awoke and forgot the dream immediately. It was not mine to know, and when the next day I witnessed burns on Grandmother's back while she changed, I told myself that they were defects from birth. When I wiped dust from the attic, a falling curtain revealing a painting of the family with a tiny ballerina in the background, I quickly replaced the fabric to hide it away. Grandmother's story should remain safe in her mind forever.

In the days it took for me to settle into living on constant alert, spring finally arrived. It was barely noticeable at first, the quiet lengthening of days and softening of wind were mere hints that spring was on its way. Spring's presence was truly confirmed, when in early April, I finished my workday in the usual evening hour, to discover the vibrant sun stretching its rays all over the city after a long slumber. It was on this day that I felt a rapid mood switch, the sun cleansing me from my shame, inviting me to take a longer walk through the large park behind the building before returning to my quarters. For the first time, I could walk to my quarters while the sun was still awake.

The main building was closer to a castle than a normal residence, five storeys in height plus turrets extending upwards, weathervanes of oxidised, green metal pointing sharply to the sky, as if swords to engage passing clouds in battle. Gargoyles wrapped their tails around the turrets, sitting and watching from their comfortable places on top of the arches on the building's grand windows. On the top floor, which

I knew was unoccupied as I frequently removed cobwebs from its dusty corners, the glass windows were made up of stained, colourful squares depicting old battle myths. They showcased, no doubt, lies about how this family came to their riches, that they were descendants of those who had fought bravely for these lands. I knew better now. The residence's north and south faces had doors leading into a grassy terrace. The pale, red outer surfaces were pristinely cleaned, more noticeable on the north and south faces as the building was much longer than it was wide. The doors lied too, a false exit. The residence could only be exited from its east and west faces, to pass over the mossy lake on a cobblestone bridge with looped, silver rails. As I walked through the east gate, I turned back for a moment to regard two mermaid figurines who guarded the bridge on its end closest to the building. I hadn't ever noticed them before. Wishing them goodbye, I strolled into the grand park.

Seeing these surroundings in the light transformed the muted world I had grown accustomed to in the long winter. The garden was contoured and shaped pristinely, ninety-degree angles formed at the turn of each defined path, huge, evergreen trees had been planted in a row along the main road which cut the park into two. Both sides were jagged, rough edges and perfectly trimmed, rectangular hedges. It was a flawless entry into a grand building, and I marvelled guiltily, knowing that it took an entire village of people to keep the grounds maintained. Picking a path at random, I wandered like a grand visitor, as if having nowhere better to be and nothing better to do. The wind was adorned with the sound of birds, chirping above me, and rustling of bushes as Eurasian magpies with their silver-blue striped wings dived in and out, shaking the leaves. Gravel crunched under my feet, tiny rocks falling into the geometric cuts on the soles of my shoes As I lifted a foot, they fell, returning to the rest of the gravel. I looked up, noticing a woman sitting nearby.

Grandmother was dressed in a pale, yellow dress and warm scarf. She sat knitting on a bench nearby, smiling at the yarn she held. Illuminated, her hair looked as white as fresh paper. In this light her face was fresh with sun-kissed warmth, a fresh life instilled in her. It was cold, the wind often shaking the naked branches that twisted through the atmosphere above Grandmother, twigs folding into each other like wrinkles on a map. Yet she appeared unbothered by the cold, nor by her old age. Instead, she sat knitting peacefully, the returning sun shining on the blue yarn that she wrapped tightly around her knitting needle. It danced, guided by the needle, cool and calm as a stream running into a vast ocean.

Taking a long glance at the old woman, and a deep breath of icy air, I was warmed by an overwhelming gratitude for the sun. In its infiniteness, its strength, maybe it alone is the best recorder of history. Yet the sun can only see what occurs while it shines, can it not?

Perhaps it will remember Grandmother only as she was today, for she spent so much of her painful youth in the darkness. Let the sun retain the image of her peaceful figure sitting and knitting without a care in the world, for that is how she sat when it finally made her acquaintance.

Property

It never snows in New Orleans, so *you have to use your imagination*. That's what I've been told, anyway. I've never been too fond of my imagination, uneasy with the concept of a twisted reality. Why would I mess with my inner lens, my viewpoint, through which I perceive all? It would likely have dangerous consequences to fiddle with one's own mind, especially if done in excess. One could permanently sever their tether to the real world. Rest assured, I am beyond capable of inventing and creating, falsifying an image and then living in it like a dream. Yet even a most developed mind like mine struggles to generate perfect details which they have seen but not lived. I could envision a scene as if in a movie, perfect white drops hitting my skin, but I would not feel the cold simultaneously, nor admire that the very imperfections of each intricate snowflake elevate the beauty of the view altogether. I would lack the joy of noticing the larger flakes fall slowly as the wind caught onto their surface. There would be an image, certainly, but no soul attributed. As the creator I cannot be surprised by my own vision. What good would imagining snow give me? I can stare at a picture of

121

snow for days and yet no piece of art, no play and no poem can be properly comprehended without the minimum level of physical engagement that I lack access to. Thus, I have not lived the experience of snow. I likely never will.

The last time I tried to mention this, I was promptly hushed by my mother. It turned out that my aunt was horrified, spilling the glass of wine she'd been holding and pouring red liquid all over our vintage carpet. The stain never came out. She'd inquired if I was ill and an excuse was made; *I have a headache, I'm too stressed at work* or such other. I have since noted that these kinds of thoughts should only be shared with certain special members of the population, the strong-hearted that ponder about the layers between humans and their reality. Aunt Maia was clearly not this sort of person. She probably never craved snow, never longed for the forbidden like I do. Yet you are a most different sort, the type who has seen me pierce my own soul and bleed out before you, not twitching an eye nor trembling a lip at the complex ideas I hold within myself. You, who loves the snow, must love hearing about it. It's something I believe without ever having asked. My certainty reinforces itself, a dangerous loop. I'd like to say that a person could not be this certain without hitting their hammer on the nail of truth, and yet thinking this way could amplify a lie all the same. I must tread carefully. However, you do not shake your head at me, my love. I must continue then in my assumption that you are content.

I digress. Where was I? Oh, quite right, my dear. I was just about to describe our first meeting. My favourite story.

It was a particularly cold day, the kind that makes a person doubt the weather forecast for a moment and think there might be potential for snow. Clear skies were predicted, yet huge, defined clouds hung low, burdened by their own weight. These clouds were far too divine to be the object of a children's game, no one could guess that they were shaped like anything other than clouds themselves. These clouds were so vibrantly heavy that they carved out their own impression. After my regular, tiring shift at the accounting firm I work at, I walked under the grey sky through the old square, past Mickey's teahouse. As I passed, Mickey himself took a step onto the sidewalk and waved. I waved back, as is routine with Mickey. That insufferable, old stranger who feels an odd attachment to me due to circumstances far beyond my control. I would ask, *who cares if you held me as an infant*, as a stranger in my life when the expression of consent was unfathomable, let alone its withdrawal. I certainly would have refused if I could. I have learnt, also through difficult measures, that I am not allowed to ask such questions.

After the encounter with Mickey, I found my social battery quite drained for the day. My feet, sensing this, moved without concern for my conscious mind, turning down a small alleyway to avoid the crowds. It was a shortcut of a different sense - a longer walk in distance but a shorter one in time as I avoided pushing through groups of teenagers and children winding through my feet like lost guinea pigs in the wild, mountainous countryside of Peru. Upon entering this alleyway, I was quite struck by the realisation that a repeated noise was coming from the distance. It was a thumping of sorts, like the soft ticking of a watch's second hand. As I followed my wayward feet, who had overtaken me in their desire to follow this noise, I sped past old buildings, shrubs growing down the rails of their decorated balconies, and turned a corner into a small street whose existence I was not previously aware of. Could you imagine that? I, a local, had not ventured there before. If I had, we would have met earlier. It is a deep regret of mine that I had never passed my usual turn and followed that foreign path a while longer, just to see what was there.

The primitive cold was fearless here, and the spitting wind threw me into the second door on my left upon making the turn. It was a square-shaped antique store, lacking in room for the great number of tiny treasures it contained. Painted porcelain ornaments were stuffed into every crevice of each dusty shelf. An entire wall was dedicated to cuckoo clocks with intricacies carved in and out of the wood. Mismatched tea set pieces, the fragile ones wrapped in pink doilies, were grouped together, with knives, rings, and other various sparkling, silver metals scattered around them. A Scottish woman looked at me curiously, asking if I was looking for anything specific. She had silver streaks in her dark hair, which streamed down her cropped shirt and over her naked stomach, reaching the curve of her waist. The woman was adorned with gemstones and colours from head to toe, and both the gum she was chewing, her accent, and my fascination for her unique appearance, meant that I did not hear her question the first time it was asked.

I can't recall my exact words, but I distinctly remember asking her to show me something of unrivalled beauty. *Something she would be sad to part with.* The sound of thumping returned as she led me past rows of cabinets, each containing more exquisite, sparkling novelties. The noise grew louder, and louder, as we walked through the never-ending store. Gone was the previous tiny, cramped space. I had entered another world entirely, surrounded by the serenity of past-loved baubles and a distant grandmother's wooden spoons. Nothing, however, could have compared me to the feeling of laying my eyes on a figure as perfect as you.

Don't blush, my dear. In my mind it is true, and what do we care about others' realities? Let mine be the objective one while I tell this story. You are, as you will be forever, exquisite. Separate from all other creatures, all other items a person could possess, you were not born but instead designed with pristine perfection in mind.

A beautiful ballerina, trapped in a cage of thick glycerine and confetti to resemble snow. A ceramic skirt resembling white tulle, and a strapless top with a heart-shaped neckline that clung tightly to the skin.

Hair wrapped in a round bun at the top of the head, without a single flyaway strand. Such smooth skin, each detail up to the curve of your nails so lifelike that I began to see your fingers swim through the liquid and touch the snow. Unlike the ballerina, the base of the snow globe glittered with colourful, shimmering patterns. Blue, purple, white and gold outlined frost flakes and snowmen were drawn in stunning realism.

The shopkeeper informed me that you were on discount because your creator, a young, rising Italian artist, had not finished the details of the ceramic before his sudden and unpredicted death. It was related to gang violence, but the snow globe escaped being captured as evidence. Despite the idea that this would be a historic selling-point, many claimed that you possessed a tainted, unlucky energy. They couldn't have been more wrong. Without being painted by another, you were fit into the snow globe's base and put up for sale yet avoided for years due to superstition. I knew immediately that you were simply destined to wait for me. You and I are wanderers, misunderstood souls who had been searching for each other all our lives. The only curse that we face is the curse of being misplaced, surrounded by those who cling to the mainstream for fear of the unknown. We, my dear, relish the unknown. We thrive in the darkness, beyond the borders that others do not dare to cross.

What you awoke in me was a desire to live unburdened. I suddenly realised the entrapment of my very own hot flesh, blood storming through my heart, shrieking like a drunk man begging for a taste to forget his own mortality. Each beat prayed for another sip. My yearning muscles, my frail body that would never feel perfection like you could. You might have once been considered a belonging, something to be created and bought and sold, but are we humans not the ones guilty of purchasing each other? When humans hurt one another, we live in blind ignorance of the fact that we are the disposable ones. If my bones were to break, I could not sparkle eternally like you would. I would return to the Earth and start again, leaving no trace of my life behind.

When I stared at you in the store, listening to our united, even breaths, I understood that we are equally unable to bend before we shatter. The thumping noise returned, loud like a drum inside my ear.

It was your heart. I could hear your heart beating in perfect rhythm with my own. Time was no longer real.

I have no more memories of the store woman, of taking you home, of anything other than the days I have spent since, staring at you as the picture of serenity. The rosiness of your cheeks in the cold and dull of the snow globe. Your vibrant skin, your hair coming undone and kissing your bare shoulders in the wind. I watch you dance, spinning and jumping ceaselessly. You are all that is beautiful in this world, an ever-still, pristine image. My love, my perfection. I have not tired of you since.

Is it not a wonderful story, my love? Does hearing it make you long for me once more? Do not act callous anymore, I have missed your voice for so long. Lately, you have not been speaking to me, you have not been dancing in my dreams as you used to. I am incapable of losing my love for you, my desire unfaltering. Yet now, as I sit and wait in anguish for your response, I feel time engulf me once more and pull me back to reality. I have tried to be patient; I have tried to set aside my longing, but I cannot bear this any longer. Perhaps I was naive to believe the story would break your indifference, that reminding you of my feelings would bring a heart into one who was designed without one.

Is that what you have wanted all along? To take the one who loves you, the one who owns you, and overpower him? Take advantage of the pure love of your master, shame him in his own home? You, who was nothing before my gaze, stuck in that maze of a store, stared at by strangers like a zoo animal! You, who would continue to be trapped without me, without my selfless enchantment!

I have waited long enough now; I demand a reply! I demand it! Answer me at once! Answer or suffer the consequences!

So, she does not speak. I see the wickedness of your heart to lie to me, betray me thoughtlessly, ignore me as soon as my vulnerabilities have been shown. You witch! Have you no shame at the things you have made me feel, only to rip them from my tender fingers and leave scalds in their place? There is evil in your unspoken words, in a glimmering eye that watches silently. Illusions of comprehension fade away and I am suddenly aware that I am reflected in the glass of the snow globe. You have shown me what I wanted to see, and now that you have secured your place in my heart you wish to take this away from me. So, this is your game then. I won't let you win! Property can have no place over man in this world. I will smash you to bits, witch! Watch you writhe across my floor, your beauty cracked and worthless. Your talents, your dance, they die tonight, by my side. I was the one destined to enjoy them, and so I will have my last dance!

Vessels

"Let me love you like we are young again, still nostalgic for the all-encapsulating warmth of the womb, of nurture that is given without asking for a return. No strings, the first love begs you to only be alive."

Part I - Elina

When the racing thoughts of the human mind are sufficiently limited, we unburden ourselves from the stress of trivialities. Appearances, social anxiety. A fresh cup of coffee spilt on a silk blouse gifted by an elderly aunt that expects to see it worn. It doesn't seem as consequential of an issue if both are busy enough to forget the blouse in the first place. At least, that's what I'd like to imagine, that the more I constrain my thoughts the less they will consume me.

So far, this hypothesis lacks an empirical basis. Twenty-two years of life, and still I have not found a way to stop every tiny, superficial idea from devouring my mind. Whether employed or job-hunting, beginning or completing studies, surrounded by people or entirely alone, tension accompanies me through every situation. The most recurring of the agitating thoughts is the issue of my skin. It is increasingly common nowadays that people are born without it, bare lumps of flailing fibre and tissue, screaming from raw, little lungs as they exit the womb missing the largest organ in their body. The most recent estimate is that roughly one in 1,000 is affected by the condition. I would guess that exact statistic, while correct on a global scale, does not account for the distribution of us. I am one of very few in the city of Copenhagen, or so it feels.

Today I receive more stares than usual. It is early in the evening yet dark, as the sun wishes the city goodbye during the early afternoon, the pathways are illuminated only by warm, orange-toned hues of streetlamps and the sharp, white light from the smartphones of those wading through it. I hobble down the cobblestone pathway, puddles of a past rain loosening the grip of my shoes on the path. I fear falling, of slipping and landing on my eye which never closes. Today I should have worn the suit, I think to myself. My hands are the only covered part of me, for practical purposes I need to be able to type on the computer keyboard at work. We have a sufficiently strict non-discrimination policy in place for the skinless, so I don't mind being myself there. For the public, it is important to remember my fake skin. It makes getting around easy. I would have gone directly home at 17:00, but it is Harry's birthday in a week, and I need to get him a gift. Reluctantly, I wobble along the slick road to the bookstore, past delicate balconies on pastel buildings of equal height. They are lined with wooden frameworks, purposefully exposed to give the feel of ancient history that has been pristinely preserved. I could not contrast more with the perfect, little, old city if I'd tried.

Thankful to reach the bookstore without injury, I step forward and push the glass door overzealously. The bottom edge hits into a stopper while its hinges prevent the door from bending backwards into the wrong direction, and a clang echoes through the bookstore mockingly, notifying everyone that some clumsy dork has pushed a *pull* door. An elderly woman browsing through the yellow sale signs by the entrance looks up from her pages fearfully, as if never having heard such a terrifying noise in all her seventy-or-so years of life. I pull the door and creep inside, while she continues watching me. Walking past her in hunt for the history section, a realisation pops into my mind but I push it away. I am already too sapped of energy from the passing week to batter myself further with negative talk. Instead, running my fingers over the colourful books, I read every title and author out in my mind and admire the varying fonts on the books' spines. One catches my eye. I am sure I have heard Harry mention this author before. I edge the book off a high shelf and catch it in my outstretched hands, feeling its weight as I bring it close enough to read. I note the elegant cover design as I read the back cover, as well as the first four pages of the introduction to check for a cohesive, strong tone. Harry isn't a particularly poetic person. He prefers when things get straight to the point. A slow and uncertain voice would put him off the book.

He won't wait for you forever. A voice lingers. *You know how much he puts up with for you anyway.*

The worst of the disruptive thoughts come from ones based in truth. They hurt the most, because the only way to push them back is with impotent denial, and my supply of denial seems limited these days. I walk to the counter with the book. The old woman has stopped staring now, and the cashier smiles but won't meet my eyes. People only look at me with morbid curiosity, the same way drivers stop to check on roadkill. Curiosity, like denial, isn't infinite. When they look away, when they've had enough, they'll drive away feeling sick.

Inside the book lies a poem. I read it on the train during my journey home, wondering if it was rooted in truth.

The men I know do not like pomegranates.
They have teeth that snap
and knuckles that pop.
Their large hands get in the way of disassembling.

To disassemble is to understand
how one was assembled.
View the body as more than a tool,
to be used
to conquer or dominate.

They pull and rip at the flesh of the gem
until its shine has been covered by red.
The violent burst of the seeds,
of a life.

A life that women know to search for
and men know to destroy
with their tearing fingers.

The pomegranate becomes a battlefield
its body is no longer art.
All the destroyed look the same.

Part II - Harry

We have stopped in the middle of the street, two people standing between rows of perfect, parallel trees and newly renovated buildings equidistant from the walking path. It is a chill September afternoon, a rapid cool settling in after the day's warmth. Leaves are not yet yellowing and browning, still showing off their fresh green. The sun winks from above, no rain yet dampening the ground. It is an autumn period nearly indistinguishable from the summer, except for the falling temperatures.

Elina looks up at me, her unlidded eye rolling in its socket, optic nerve angling to deliver my image to her brain. Her skinless face is lit by the fresh remains of light, emotion spotlighted despite her best attempt to hide it. She doesn't say anything at first, but I hear her heart's rhythm change, beats speeding up as the organ's walls push blood harder to her body. Each thump is louder, more forceful, communicating her inner thoughts to me. Something is wrong. When I try to look towards the beating organ between her lungs, she covers herself instinctively with a fleshy arm.

"What are you nervous about?" I ask, motioning at her chest.

"Oh, it's nothing."

"Hey, you can tell me!" I smile. "Is something bothering you, Elina?"

"I... I'm cold," she stammers, taking a rapid breath. Her lungs stretch to fill themselves with air, encaged by her ribs. Uncovered like this, they appear so brittle and she, so vulnerable. A harsh word carried on the wind could whittle away at her, my very breath could reach in and carve out her insides, tearing her apart if I commanded it to. I let our communication happen on her terms, give her some control amidst this unpredictable and frightening life. It is a power itself to rebuild, rather than destroy. To put aside my hold on her, my knowledge of her insecurity, and instead let her have all the autonomy she chooses. It is my privilege to do so for her.

Despite Elina's best efforts to hide, I can hear the heart pulsating with blood, walls of muscle thumping. Her heart sounds like it is at war, every movement an unabating fight to grasp life itself for one more second. One more beat.

"Oh," I say, thinking of a solution. Naturally, effortlessly, as if letting my guard down is the easiest thing in the world, I begin to stretch my fingertips. My nail hunts for the gap between the seams of my artificial skin.

"I'm sorry. I know this was meant to be our day out, but I forgot the rest of my skin, I was in such a rush. I really wanted to..." she trails off as she notices what I am doing. She knows exactly what is happening, yet it doesn't stop the incoming question.

"Harry, what are you doing?"

I finally grasp the edge of the costume and begin to stretch my skin off. There is a pull, and a vague pain as I detach from the shell. Finger by finger, a single hand has been removed. Then the second, and here a connecting stitch gets stuck, and I untangle it as Elina observes with curiosity.

I take her hand from her chest, careful to protect the exposed parts of her from overstimulation. I place the gloves into the hand. My shed skin acts as a conduit between us. It lets me love her gently, thoughtfully, just as I wish to do. Knowing that I can keep her safe and warm is enough to bring me joy. Knowing that I can enjoy another smile with her, share another laugh, another conversation that makes the world around us glow with wonder.

"Harry..." There is a newfound softness to her voice, each syllable sliding into my ear like the roll of sweet honey on her tongue. Elina looks at me, her eyes pooled with human understanding. We know each other. It is a sentiment far beyond love and limerence.

"There's more. Tell me what parts of you are cold."

She stares at me in a tender trance, unable to form a reply.

"What parts, Elina? Your neck?" I hover my bare fingertips just outside the base of her neck, the curve where it meets her shoulder, and she tenses. There is heat here. I trace the air and move down her arm, still not touching her. I can't, and yet I don't need to, the sound of her heart and her shallow breaths echoing in her neck are my signs.

"Your arm, then?" I pull again at myself, unsticking from my exterior further. My bicep aches, the coat is most secure as I reach towards vital areas.

"This is already... too much... I don't... I can't..." she gushes as I wrap the skin around her arms. It adjusts so naturally as if my body was meant to be hers from the very beginning, the amalgamating of perfectly compatible vessels. She doesn't stop me from weaving my skin into her.

"Better?" She will lie in her answer, yet I ask anyway.

"Much, yes."

"No, it's not," I chuckle, "Elina, that can't have been enough to warm you up."

"I can't accept this-" Saliva has pooled on her tongue and she presses it against the roof of her mouth to gulp the liquid down. I take this opportunity to cut her off mid-sentence.

"I would do far more for you. If you had asked, instead of pointlessly apologising, I would have given it to you hours ago. If I knew you were uncomfortable, Elina I would have-"

"You shouldn't have to do anything. It was my mistake."

To another person her face would be expressionless, she lacks a lip to quiver or eyelid to bat. I feel her warmth instead, the fluster manifesting in her heated face. I sense the darting of her eyes and unsettled twitch of her finger from the way air bends around her. I know her words and better yet, every dip in her voice and twitch of her tongue. Beyond what she says, I know what she means.

"I would give you all but my face. I don't want to see myself when I admire you."

"You admire this?" she murmurs shyly. "You enjoy looking at me, even like this?"

"Why wouldn't I?"

"I look like a monster, Harry. To everyone."

"Any person that would limit humanity to your exterior, does not know what it means to be human at all. You are more of a person to me than anyone else I have met."

She doesn't have a response for this, so I continue to layer her in my skin until her vitals calm.

"Elina?" At hearing her own name, she trembles. I continue, "does it scare you to see me like this?"

"Of course not."

"Good." I pause. "Should we continue our walk then?"

"Yes, let's." Her voice lightens as if she was smiling.

I look at her face once more, completely naked. She is flesh and muscle and bone. She is a bare soul entirely exposed, no secrets or deceit. A fresh gust of air ties us together, her brown eyes deep and lovely, filled with knowing. She can read my mind now, as my face refuses to hide the single thought I have at witnessing her raw beauty. *I love you, Elina.* I want to tell her. She starts talking, afraid to hear it.

"I'm sorry for being so difficult."

"Do you love me, Elina?"

"Of course I do."

"Then it's enough." My voice is decisive and clear.

"It's enough?"

"Beyond enough. Far beyond. Don't project your fears onto me. Let me love you. Let me enjoy your existence, laugh with you, miss my train on purpose to sit at the platform talking with you until the next arrives. It's you and me, Elina. More than enough."

She gasps, shocked. Yet I watch her relax, her shoulder blades separate, and her knees click in anticipation. I hear her heartbeat soften and I crave her further, wanting to show her more love than has existed in the world before. She is my joy, all my desires, standing just an arm's reach away.

We continue our walk.

Part III - Elina

Harry stands in the kitchen, peeling a pomegranate while I watch. The marble countertop is splattered with droplets of red, the pomegranate juice covering his hands and face. He wears a relaxed yet focused expression on his face as a finger sinks into the fruit's flesh and out pop many vibrant seeds. His hands are gentle as if he is handling a baby animal, recognising the senses of the pomegranate. There is no tearing, no harsh clawing to excavate the insides of the fruit. No, he does not take for granted the power, the state he has over the pomegranate's fragile nerves. Instead, Harry unfolds the skin with a soft lovingness. Life transforms in his hands. He handles the fruit like it is the most important thing this world has to give, and I am warm with the wonder of us sharing this moment. I savour the view of his furrowing brow, lip bit in concentration, mind busy navigating his steady hands.

I feel an understanding of the way the world grants us joys, and how we must treat them. Once the act is done, he steps towards me and smiles with the same heartfelt seriousness that he gave to the pomegranate. As if secretly telling me *I can do it. I want to love you the way only stars are capable of.*

It is as if I am the pomegranate, his joy, his lovely world.

For him I would turn into a softer creature, transform and let him handle me. Let my guard down and be nothing more than a resting being. I would let him handle me, peel me open. We are made of the same soul anyway. It has long been so, even if I did not know, did not realise until he showed me exactly that beneath our skin our hearts could beat in unison. Watching him peel the pomegranate, I understand.

I love you.